Kidnapped in Sweden

Roy MacGregor

An M&S Paperback Original from
McClelland &
The Cana

An M&S Paperback Original from
McClelland & Stewart Inc.

Canadian Cataloguing in Publication Data
MacGregor, Roy, 1948–
    Kidnapped in Sweden

(The Screech Owls series)
"An M&S paperback original."
ISBN 0-7710-5615-X

I. Title. II. Series: MacGregor, Roy, 1948–   .
The Screech Owls series.

PS8575.G84K52 1997   jC813'.54   C97-931040-7
PZ7.M4Ki 1997

We acknowledge the financial support of the Government of
Canada through the Book Publishing Industry Development
Program for our publishing activities. We further acknowledge
the support of the Canada Council for the Arts and the Ontario
Arts Council for our publishing program.

Cover illustration by Gregory C. Banning
Typeset in Bembo by M&S, Toronto

Printed and bound in Canada

McClelland & Stewart Inc.
The Canadian Publishers
481 University Avenue
Toronto, Ontario
M5G 2E9

3 4 5 6 7   04 03 02 01 00

To Oscar and Jacob Leander-Olsson, two great hockey fans, and their father, Hans-Inge, whose help was so willingly offered and so gratefully received.

And to NHL star Daniel Alfredsson, who helped with the translations.

ACKNOWLEDGEMENTS

The author is grateful to Doug Gibson, who thought up this series, and to Alex Schultz, who pulls it off.

"EEEE–AWWW–KEEE!"

The moment Travis Lindsay heard the ridiculous yell, he closed his eyes and shook his head. It meant the Screech Owls' big defenceman, Wayne Nishikawa, had come up with a new call.

"EEEE–AWWW–KEEE!"

Nish had certainly been this loud before. He'd screamed worse when he fell through the ice on his snowmobile when the Owls had gone up north, and he'd yelped in real terror that day at summer hockey camp when he'd gone skinny dipping with the snapping turtle. But the biggest difference was that this time Nish's call was filled with joy rather than horror.

Nish, stripped naked again in the middle of a lake, was having the time of his life.

"EEEE–AWWW–KEEE!"

This time, however, the lake was frozen solid, and Nish *wanted* the world to see him! This time he was fully expected to have absolutely nothing on, and this time he didn't have to worry about drowning or an attack from a snapping turtle!

Did they have snapping turtles in Sweden? Travis wondered.

He shivered. He, too, was bare naked, and on a day so cold he couldn't even breathe through his nose. If they did have snapping turtles, Travis thought, there was nothing to worry about today. If one was hiding anywhere around here, it would be suffering from lockjaw, frozen solid!

Travis couldn't believe how quickly the air could change from unbearable heat to unbearable cold. A moment ago the sweat had been pouring off his face so fast it seemed as if Lars Johanssen, the Owls' nifty little defenceman, had dumped the bucket of water over Travis's head instead of over the white-hot rocks of the club sauna. The water had sizzled and steamed and the temperature had risen so dramatically that Travis had trouble breathing.

Now, standing outdoors, naked and skinny as the birch trees that grew down to the edge of this frozen Scandinavian lake, he had trouble breathing again. Travis's nostrils were frozen shut. He was breathing through his mouth and the air was coming out in a fog as thick as the exhaust from his father's car when they headed out for an early-morning practice back in Canada.

Travis looked around him. Except for Nish and Lars Johanssen, most of the Screech Owls – Data Ulmar, Willie Granger, Andy Higgins, Jesse Highboy, Dmitri Yakushev, Gordie Griffith,

Derek Dillinger, Fahd Noorizadeh, Jeremy Weathers, Wilson Kelly, Mike Romano, the new third-line winger – were all still huddled next to the sauna building, their hands wrapped around their naked bodies like too-small blankets.

The Owls looked ridiculous. They were trying to use the building to shield themselves from the wind. Steam was rising from their heads and shoulders the way Travis had once seen it curl up from the team of horses that had drawn the Owls around the maple-sugar bush that belonged to Sarah Cuthbertson's grandparents.

Sarah was here. Well, not *here* – not *now*, with crazy Nish standing bare naked out in the middle of the lake. But she was here in Stockholm.

Sarah would return to her own team after the tournament. Her parents thought the trip would be an excellent opportunity for her to get a feel for the larger Olympic-sized ice surface, where Sarah hoped to play for the Canadian women's team one day.

Sarah and the other girls on the team – Liz Moscovitz, Chantal Larochelle, and Jenny Staples – had all gone off with the Stockholm women's team. For all Travis knew, the girls were going through the same strange ritual.

"Normally," Sarah had said on the bus ride out into the countryside from their hotel near the Globen Arena, "it would be boys and girls together."

"*Naked?*" Nish had asked, his eyes widening.

"Of course, *naked*," Sarah had laughed. "You think they wear full hockey equipment into the sauna?"

"No, but . . ."

"You've got to loosen up, Nishikawa. You're too uptight about everything."

It would be hard to call Nish uptight at the moment, Travis thought. *Crazy*, maybe. Or *insane*.

Nish was standing well out from the shore, a pink hamster in a sea of white. He was using one hand to cover himself and the other to wave at the cars driving by on the far side of the bay. They were, Travis thought, too far away to see him — fortunately!

Lars, who used to live in Sweden, had been the first to break from the pack and go running, barefoot, across the lake and jump straight into the freezing water through the gaping hole in the ice.

Nish, of course, had to be second. One steaming, churning bare-naked butt hurling across the open ice, still waving at the passing cars.

"*It's a breakaway!*" Wilson shouted.

"*Go, Nish! Go!*" they called.

Nish ran towards the open water, where Lars was already splashing about. He leapt and screamed once more before landing, like a pink beluga, in a mammoth splash of black water.

"EEEE–AWWW–KEEE!"

TRAVIS FELT INCREDIBLY ALIVE – WHICH WAS quite odd, because only a few moments earlier he had been convinced he was dead.

Ever since the sauna and the plunge into the freezing lake, Travis felt as if every pore of his skin had been drilled and flushed and buffed. He sizzled with energy, sparked with new life. Just as Lars had said he would. He felt like he was wearing a brand-new skin, and it was a skin with so much jump in it that, well, he couldn't possibly be the same old Travis Lindsay.

In a way, he figured, he wasn't. The Travis Lindsay who had landed at Stockholm's international airport the day before had come to doubt his own courage, especially when it came to hockey. He had always worried about his own bravery; he still preferred a night light when he was home. But a month ago, in a league game, he had gone down to block a shot from the point and the big shooter had held on too long so that, by the time he shot, it was Travis's face, not his shin pads, that blocked the way to the net. The shot had ripped the cage right off his helmet, and one of the broken screws had cut him just over the eye for two stitches.

Now he was afraid. He flinched whenever anyone took a hard shot in his direction. He was afraid to go down and block the puck. No one – with the possible exception of Muck Munro, the Screech Owls' coach – suspected anything, but Travis knew something was different. And he was secretly delighted that he'd been able to race across that ice bare naked and jump into the open water. At least he still had *some* guts.

Maybe this trip was just what he needed to get right again. So far, it was going perfectly.

Mr. Johanssen had come to the team with the idea. Sweden was hosting the first International Goodwill Pee Wee Tournament, with games in Stockholm, Gothenburg, and Malmö. Mr. Johanssen's lumber manufacturing company was one of the main tournament sponsors, and it had been suggested to him that a team from North America might give the tournament a truly international feel. Almost like a mini-World Cup!

Mr. Johanssen's company agreed to sponsor the Screech Owls, and the head office in Stockholm was able to arrange a special deal with SAS airlines. Before anyone quite realized what was happening, the Owls and most of their parents were all packing for Sweden.

Even Muck was going. The parents went to him with a proposition: if he could arrange the time off, they'd pick up the cost of his flight and accommodation. He couldn't refuse, even though Travis and Nish and some of the other long-time Owls thought he'd like nothing better. He kept grumbling about what his old hockey buddies would say if they found out he was going to Don Cherry's least-favourite hockey country.

No one paid the slightest attention to Muck's protests. Mr. Lindsay booked him on the flight and that was that. There would be no turning back. The team was delighted: no way did they want to play anywhere, not even practise, without Muck as their coach.

Teams were coming from Helsinki and Turku in Finland, and from Oslo in Norway. A German team was entered, a team from the Czech Republic, and, as a last-minute entry, a team was coming all the way from Russia.

Not only that, but the Russian team was from Moscow, and from the same CSKA club that had produced such superstars as Pavel Bure and Alexander Mogilny and Sergei Fedorov. What's more, it would have Dmitri Yakushev's first cousin playing on it. According to Dmitri – and later confirmed by Mr. Johanssen, who checked into it – his cousin, Slava Shadrin, was considered to be the best peewee player in all of Russia. Or, as Dmitri, who rarely, if ever, bragged, put it: "the best peewee player Russia has *ever* produced."

"Hardly," said Travis, who was a great fan of Bure's.

"That's what my uncle says – and he should know."

Dmitri's uncle was Alexander Yakushev, the great scoring star of the 1972 Summit Series between the Soviet Union and Team Canada, so perhaps he would know. But still, Travis found it hard to believe anyone could say something like that about a *kid*.

"How old is he?" Travis had asked Dmitri one practice before they boarded the plane that would fly them to Copenhagen and then on to Stockholm.

"Thirteen, I think."

"Well, how can they say such things about a thirteen-year-old? How can they know?"

"You're Canadian, aren't you?" Dmitri had asked.

Travis was caught off guard. "Yeah, of course. What's that mean?"

"Didn't you ever read any books about Wayne Gretzky or Bobby Orr?"

"Yeah, sure."

"Well, when *they* were thirteen, people knew, didn't they?"

Travis supposed they did. He could hardly wait to see this new Russian sensation. He was half excited at the prospect of seeing someone who must certainly be headed for the NHL, half terrified at the thought of having to play against him. What if he was also a centre? What if Travis had to take the face-offs against him? No . . . Sarah was back. Travis would be moved back to left wing.

The boys were getting ready to head out to the bus when Muck and Mr. Lindsay came in.

"Let's go!" Muck shouted. "You're on in an hour!"

"On the bus?" Fahd asked.

Muck rolled his eyes.

"You're on the bus in five, mister. You're on the ice in an hour."

"*Ice* – where?" Travis couldn't help himself. They hadn't skated since they got there, and everyone was excited about checking out the big European ice surface.

"Globen rink," Muck said, giving away nothing.

The Screech Owls couldn't believe it. One day in Sweden and they were off to skate in the magnificent Globen Arena.

Where the Maple Leafs' Mats Sundin had played for Djurgårdens.

Where Peter Forsberg's MoDo team from Ornskoldsvik had come to play.

Where the World Championships had been played.

Where the Screech Owls were on in an hour.

3

THE SCREECH OWLS WERE LINED UP TO GO ON.
The ice was glistening in the bright lights of the
Globen Arena. Travis looked up through his
mask: the building was a perfect circle, the roof
high and white and domed, the walls curving
down, and bright red seats everywhere. It was the
strangest hockey rink Travis had ever seen.

"It's like the inside of a golf ball," Sarah said.
She was also looking up.

"It's beautiful," said Travis.

And huge. Muck explained to them that the
ice surface was only fifteen feet – five adult steps
– wider than they were used to, and that there
was no difference at all in length. "But it will *feel*
longer," he said. "The nets are farther out from
the boards, and the corners deeper."

But even Muck's warning had not prepared
them for the sensation of the bigger ice surface.
Travis hit the fresh ice, did his special stutter step
to pick up speed, leaned down to stare at his
skates as they marked fresh ice, and felt as if he
was skating once again on James Bay, with the ice
stretching as far as the eye could see.

He could hear his blades. It was almost as if they were thanking him for the magnificent ice. All he had to do was take a stride and he could feel the blades dig in; all he had to do was push off and he could sense the light snow spraying off as his skate dug deeper and flicked.

Travis lifted his head slightly so he could see the traffic ahead of him. Sarah Cuthbertson was skating so effortlessly her blades seemed to sigh while everyone else's sizzled. She floated over the ice surface, somehow capable of picking up speed even when she was gliding.

Travis smiled to himself as he watched her skate. Often, the Owls played teams whose best skaters — always boys, always the team stars — would seethe with such envy they would throw their own games off as they tried to show Sarah up. They would chase her around as if the game were tag, not hockey. And when they couldn't catch her, they would trip her. Sarah was really like two players in one: one to set up the goals for the Screech Owls, and one to draw the penalties from the opposition.

Travis passed Muck, who was skating in his old windbreaker and wearing the old gloves that some of the Owls figured dated from Columbus's discovery of America, or whenever it was that Muck played junior hockey before a broken leg shattered his dreams of playing in the National Hockey League.

Muck was skating with a man Travis had never seen before. He was tall and blond and was wearing a blue-and-yellow track suit with three small golden crowns on the front. He was a big man, and rocked on his skates as he moved, the blades effortlessly tossing a spray of ice on every lift – the sign of a very, very strong skater. He was wearing his hair in a style Travis had never seen before. He could tell it was gelled, for it glistened in the Globen lights, and it stuck up in a series of odd spikes. It was different, Travis thought, and kind of, well, *neat*.

Muck and the blond man skated to centre ice, where Muck blew once on his whistle.

The Owls converged on centre ice.

Muck might as well have been in the arena back home. He had his same old clothes on. Same old gloves and stick and whistle. And, as usual, he had the Owls' full attention.

Muck was unlike any coach Travis had ever known. No shouting "*Listen up!*" No fancy clipboards or plastic ice surfaces and felt-tip pens. Only Muck, talking.

"This here is Borje Salming," he said.

The man smiled. His smile was crooked, his lips and face heavily scarred, as if he'd been carved out of a tree with a chainsaw. But the smile was warm, and the blue eyes danced with friendliness under the gelled hair.

"You want to tell the boys who Mr. Salming is, Lars?"

Lars cleared his throat. Even he had been caught off guard.

"F-former Toronto Maple Leaf and Detroit Red Wing. Defence. First Swedish player named to the Hockey Hall of Fame."

"That's pretty good!" laughed Borje Salming.

Willie Granger, the team's trivia expert, pushed forward and spoke up.

"Six times named to the NHL All-Star team – 150 goals, 637 assists, 787 points."

Salming's eyes widened in surprise. "That's *very* good!"

"Mr. Johanssen's company has arranged for Mr. Salming to spend a practice with each of the teams playing in this tournament," Muck explained. "He and his assistants will be working with you this afternoon."

"ALL-RIGHHHTTTTT!" Willie shouted.

"YES!" shouted Lars.

No one had to turn to see who it was calling loudest from the back.

"EEEE–AWWW–KEEE!"

Travis had never thought a practice could be like this. He had been playing now for six years and had been skating since he was three. But today he felt he knew nothing.

There were three other Swedish coaches to help Borje Salming. One of them, an older man with glasses and a beard, had a clipboard that held a book containing the drills they were doing.

They skated for several minutes. None of the counter-clockwise circuits with whistled speed changes that they were used to in Canada, but intricate crossovers and shifts in direction.

Borje Salming blew his whistle at centre ice, and all the Owls skated out to form a circle around him. Nish and Sarah arrived at almost the same time, and stopped at the edge of the circle.

"Nice hair, eh?" Nish giggled.

"I think he's cute," Sarah whispered back.

Nish shook his head in disgust.

Travis noticed that the other coaches were removing the nets from the ice and were bringing out four small, red, box-shaped frames.

Salming scooped up the puck with his stick. He did it the way Travis had seen other NHLers do it. Effortlessly, smoothly, the stick snaked out, snaked back, and, as if by magic, the puck was suddenly lying on the blade and then floating through the air until it landed, perfectly, in the palm of his glove. He didn't seem to be even thinking about it.

Salming held up the puck. "I don't have to tell you that the game is all about this and what you are able to do with it," he said. "But we want to show you how kids learn the game in Sweden."

He reached into his track-suit pocket, removed another puck, and held it up beside the puck he had scooped from the ice. This one was different. It was about half the size.

"We teach Swedish youngsters how to handle small pucks first," he said. "You don't give a full-size basketball to a five-year-old, do you? No matter how tall he is."

"No," Fahd said. Fahd could always be counted on to say the obvious.

"The game in Europe is all about *tempo*," Salming said. "Anyone know what I mean by 'tempo'? Anyone a musician?"

Fahd, of course, raised his hand. "I play piano."

"Well?"

"Tempo tells you how slow or fast to play the piece of music."

Salming smiled, nodding. "Same in hockey. If you can learn to do drills at full speed, then you won't even have to think about what you should be doing during a game. Little kids can't handle NHL regulation pucks the same way they can these little things. And obviously they can't shoot them the same."

He pointed to the four red frames the other coaches had set up. They faced each other in two pairs on each side of the centre red line.

"Little pucks require little nets," he said, indicating the frames. "We teach our skills this way. Young players can handle these little pucks better, and shoot them a lot better. We use the smaller nets to teach accuracy."

Salming divided the Owls into two groups, one for the pair of tiny nets at the far end of the Globen rink, one for the near end. The rules were simple: no offsides, no stoppages, be creative, take chances.

Travis had never heard such talk from a coach – not even Muck, who believed in having fun on the ice and almost always gave them a few minutes of shinny at the end of a practice. But even when they played shinny back in Canada there would be whistles, and play would be stopped, and coaches would explain mistakes. Here there would be nothing. No control. No teaching. No stopping. Nothing.

In all his hockey years, Travis had never experienced anything quite like this. It was *wonderful*! It was exciting. It was fun – more fun, he thought, than he had ever had on an ice surface.

They played in groups of three: Travis, Dmitri, and Sarah against Nish, Data, and big Andy Higgins. Borje Salming and the other coach at their end just threw the puck into the corner and the game was under way. All four coaches then formed a line across centre to stop the little pucks from crossing the centre line.

16

The pucks felt almost weightless. Travis found he could stickhandle like an NHL pro. And when he shot, it took the slightest flick of his wrist to send a snap shot hard and high off the glass. He couldn't believe it!

And yet there was no point in pounding a shot off the glass just because it sounded great. As he played and sweated and gasped for breath, Travis realized that this explained everything he had ever wondered about European hockey.

Here, on half the ice in the Globen Arena in Stockholm, with a baby puck and a toy net, he could see it all for the first time: the only way that he and Dmitri and Sarah could attack was to keep circling back and dropping the puck to each other, even if they had only half the ice surface to work with. They had to drop the puck and watch for either Nish or Data or Andy to commit themselves, allowing them a quick three-on-two. The puck was so small and light that they could pass it back and forth effortlessly and quickly, and the passing became almost hypnotic as they kept trying out new ideas. They could do anything they wanted – no whistles, no one yelling at them, no score to worry about. They circled and dropped and flicked quick little passes and kept the puck dancing on the ends of their sticks.

Scoring, however, was another matter. The net was so small that with Nish and his big shin pads in the way, it was a bit like threading a needle If they kept to the usual North American strategy they would lose possession. A shot wasn't always a safe play. Here, a shot for the sake of a shot was a waste. They had to wait, and they had to work at it so one of them would have the ideal angle. No big fancy slapshots. Quick, hard shots exactly placed – nothing else would work.

They played for nearly half an hour, and when Salming finally blew the whistle and the other coaches began to gather up the little pucks and push away the tiny nets, the Owls collapsed on their backs, sweating and puffing and giggling.

"That's *my* kind of hockey," Dmitri said.

"I *love* it!" said Sarah.

Off to the side, Nish was grunting and gasping and trying to laugh sarcastically. "One good bodycheck and you wouldn't be saying that."

Sarah laughed. "You'd have to catch us first, Big Boy."

Nish threw a glove at her. It bounced off her shoulder pads. "We won," he announced.

"Whatdya mean, 'won'?" Travis asked. "Nobody was even keeping score!"

"I *always* keep score –" Nish said.

He had barely finished speaking when his own glove flew back and bounced off his nose.

"So do I," said Sarah, giggling. "And now we're even."

4

THE SCREECH OWLS HADN'T PLAYED A SINGLE game, and yet already this was the best tournament ever. After the practice with Borje Salming and the little pucks, the lumber company Lars's father worked for was treating them to a banquet in the restaurant overlooking the ice surface, high up on the seventh floor of the Globen complex. But the Owls kept forgetting that they had come up here to eat. MoDo, one of the Swedish elite teams, was holding a practice below for their upcoming game against Djurgårdens. MoDo was Peter Forsberg's old team.

"They're playing with the little pucks!" Fahd shouted.

"They just *look* little from up here," said Travis, shaking his head at Fahd.

The meal included tiny, delicious boiled potatoes and lots of different kinds of cheese. Lars wanted them all to try the pickled herring, but he couldn't convince them that the herring wasn't a snake all curled up in the dish.

"Let me at it!" shouted Nish from another table.

Ever since the trip to James Bay, Nish fancied himself a new Man of the World. He had eaten beaver, after all — and *moose nostrils!* — so what was the big deal about a little slippery, rubbery fish?

"You eat this, Nish," Lars said, "and you get first dibs on the pudding."

Nish's eyes opened wide. "What pudding?"

"A special Swedish treat. You can go first if you eat this."

"*No prob-lem,*" Nish announced as he sat down and elaborately tucked a napkin under his chin.

He sliced off a bit of the pickled herring, sniffed it, and then began to chew.

"*Mmmmmmm,*" he kept saying. "*Ahhhhhhhhh! Per-fect!*"

Nish chewed and ate as if he'd been brought up on nothing but pickled herring. He loved a show. He loved being the centre of attention.

"You win!" said Lars. "Bring Nish some of the pudding."

Nish put down his knife and fork and dabbed at his chin, waiting, like some ancient king on his throne, for someone to serve him.

A smiling waiter came over with the special dish Lars had promised.

Nish lightly dabbed at his mouth.

"I should have some wine to clean my palate," he announced grandly.

"*You're thirteen years old!*" Fahd scolded.

"There is no drinking age in Sweden," said Nish. "Is there, Lars?"

"Well, you have to be eighteen, actually," Lars said. "But it's pretty well left up to the parents to decide when you're mature enough — which in your case would be roughly the year 2036."

Nish scowled. "*Very* funny."

The waiter placed the pudding down in front of Nish and stood back.

"*Lemme at it!*" Nish practically shouted.

"Go ahead," Lars said. "You've earned it."

Nish didn't even bother to sniff the dish. Like a front-end loader dumping snow into the back of a truck, he spooned up pudding, chewed once with his eyes closed — then stopped, his eyes opening wide!

"W-what *is* this?" he mumbled, some of the dark pudding tumbling out of his mouth.

"The English translation," said Lars, "would be 'blood pudding.' There's beer and syrup and spices mixed together with flour." He paused, grinning. "Oh yes, and the blood of a freshly slaughtered pig. It's a very old, very special Swedish recipe. It dates back hundreds and hundreds of years."

More of the dark pudding rolled out Nish's open mouth. He turned pale.

"I'MMM GONNNA HU-URLLL!"

They walked out into the brilliant sunshine of a late-winter Swedish day. Outside the Globen Hotel they waited while Nish, still spitting into a napkin, ran into the nearby McDonald's and grabbed a Big Mac to wash away the taste of the dreaded blood pudding. Then they boarded a bus for downtown.

It didn't take Nish long to recover. At the corner they passed a gas station, and Nish pointed at the signs on either side of the pumps.

"'*In*-fart'? '*Ut*-fart'?"

"'Entrance' and 'Exit,'" explained Lars, a trifle impatiently.

"Cars over here *fart* when they get gas?" Nish screamed, holding his nose.

"Very funny," Lars said. He shrugged his shoulders and moved away to the front of the bus.

Once downtown, they were all given a couple of hours to go their separate ways, promising to meet back at the bus at four o'clock.

In the sunshine, and with a light sprinkling of snow on the streets, Stockholm looked like a picture in a fairy tale. Everything seemed so old, and mysterious, and magical.

Travis and Fahd were interested in the history. They were lucky Lars was along. He told them about the canals, the churches, even a bit about the Vikings. But Nish wasn't much interested.

"EEEE–AWWW–KEEE!"

Travis winced. This hardly seemed the place for Nish to try out his new yell. They were passing a church – had he no respect?

"Eeee-awww-keee!"

The second call didn't come from Nish. It was higher pitched and distant, far off down the street.

Nish spun around in his tracks. "What was that?"

"An echo," suggested Lars.

"No way – it sounded like a *girl*!"

Nish held his hands up to his mouth to make a trumpet.

"EEEE-AWWW-KEEE!" he shouted.

"Eeee-awww-keee!" the answer came back, louder now, closer.

"They're answering me!" Nish giggled.

"Maybe they're wolves," suggested Travis.

"EEEE-AWWW-KEEE!" Nish called again.

A throng of kids was coming down the far side of the street.

One of them ran out into the street, held her hands up to her mouth, raised her head and howled, "EEEE-AWWW-KEEE!"

Nish answered back, "EEEE-AWWW-KEEE!"

The girl waved. Nish turned away, blushing.

"*They're coming over!*" he hissed.

They were Swedish, seven or eight of them in blue jackets and yellow scarves, and three or four others in ski jackets and baseball caps. They seemed like a team, or at least part of a team and their friends. The girl who had been answering Nish's call seemed very much the leader.

"Hi," she said directly to Nish. "I'm Annika. What's your name?"

Nish sputtered, and Travis couldn't blame him. Annika was so cute – perfectly blonde, with nice teeth and dimples when she smiled. But the cutest thing about her was the way she talked. When she spoke English, it was almost as if she were singing.

"N–Nish. What's yours?"

Annika giggled. "Annika. Didn't you hear me the first time or is my English no good?"

Nish was flustered. "Y-y-yeah, sure it is. I'm sorry."

"Where are you from?"

With Lars's help, Nish managed to explain all about the team and what they were doing here.

Annika's friends in the blue jackets and yellow scarves were on the Malmö peewee team. They were playing in the tournament and were in Stockholm for a game at the Globen Arena.

"Malmö?" Lars said. "We play twice in Malmö."

"Maybe against us," a tall boy said. "We've got a pretty good team."

"So do we," Nish said. "I'm assistant captain."

Travis waited for Nish to point out that he, Travis, was captain, but Nish said nothing. And

Travis couldn't figure out how to say it without sounding full of himself.

"We had a practice with Borje Salming!" Lars told them.

"*No way!*" Annika screeched.

"We did," Nish said, nodding.

"He's my all-time favourite player!" Annika said, her eyes sparking. "I still have a poster of him up in my bedroom."

"When do you go to Malmö?" the tall boy asked Travis.

"We play Russia tomorrow. I think we leave first thing the next morning."

"I'll come and watch you play," Annika said, her amazing eyes studying a blushing Nish.

"I-I'm number 21," he said.

"*Borje Salming's number!*" she yelled.

"Yeah," Nish said. "I know. He's my favourite player, too."

Travis did a double-take. How could he say that? Nish was practically a baby when Salming retired. In all the years they'd been best friends, Travis had never once heard Nish mention Borje Salming. Maybe Bobby Orr. And certainly Brian Leetch. But Salming?

"No kidding?" said Annika.

"Yeah," Nish fibbed. "Sure."

Annika held her hands up to her mouth: "EEEE–AWWW–KEEE!"

5

NEXT MORNING THEY WENT EARLY TO THE Globen Arena. Dmitri wanted to see his cousin before the game, and Travis, Lars, and Nish went along with him.

They were already flooding the ice for the Screech Owls–Russia game, but no one was in the stands. Derek's father, Mr. Dillinger, was sharpening the Owls' skates, and he waved at them from the far end of the corridor. Good ol' Mr. Dillinger.

The Russian team, CSKA, was already there, but the dressing-room door was shut tight. A man in a blue suit stood to the side, watching them. He had the sort of glasses that get darker in bright light, and they gave him a shadowed, sinister look. He had a red-and-gold CSKA pin on his jacket, so they knew he was with the team.

He answered in Russian when Dmitri addressed him. He even smiled when he realized Dmitri spoke his language, and he listened carefully, nodding and shaking his head.

Finally the man knocked on the door – two sharp quick knocks, a pause, then a third, more softly – and was admitted.

"What's the big fuss?" Nish wanted to know.

"I'm not sure," Dmitri said. "They don't seem to want anybody talking to the team. I told him I'm Slava's cousin."

"Maybe they're afraid he'll *defect*," Nish said, proud to use such a word.

Dmitri laughed. "Get with the times, Nish. Russians don't run away from home any more."

"Fedorov did. Mogilny did."

"You're talking Soviet Union, Nish. There is no more Soviet Union – or don't you pay attention in history class, either?"

"Well, why are they so nervous, then?"

A few minutes passed and the boys were getting restless. Finally the door opened and the man in the blue suit came out. Then another man, who seemed even more furtive. Then a kid. A skinny kid with slightly buck teeth and unruly blond hair.

"*Slava!*" Dmitri shouted when he saw who was coming out.

"Hey!" the other shouted, smiling.

The two boys hugged each other. Then Dmitri kissed his cousin's cheek, and Slava kissed Dmitri's cheek. Travis was standing close enough to Nish to hear him mumble, "*I'm gonna hurl.*" The cousins hugged again and then separated.

"Slava," Dmitri said. "These are my teammates. Travis, Lars, Nish, I want you to meet Viacheslav Shadrin. 'Slava' we call him."

"I don't kiss," Nish said.

Even Slava laughed. His big front teeth gave him a wonderful smile when he used it, but he didn't use it often. His English wasn't great, and Dmitri had to do a lot of translating, but the boys were able to talk about the tournament and everything they'd seen and done, including Nish's now-famous Winter Skinny Dip.

Slava nodded a lot and even laughed a couple of times, but he hadn't any stories to tell in return. Lars asked him what he'd seen and Dmitri translated, but the answer didn't amount to much apart from practice and team meetings. He hadn't shopped. He hadn't been to any of the museums.

"Ask Slava if he can come out with us in Malmö," Travis told Dmitri.

Dmitri did, but Slava only shook his head and looked forlorn. He spoke quickly to Dmitri, and he kept checking the two men from CSKA, who were talking off to the side.

"Okay," Dmitri said. "See you later, then, Slava."

Slava quickly shook their hands and turned back towards the dressing room. The man in the blue suit already had the door open. In a moment, all three had vanished inside.

"What was *that* all about?" Travis asked Dmitri.

"*In a minute*," Dmitri whispered. He waited until they had almost reached the Owls' dressing room. Then he gathered the others close.

"The man in the blue suit?" Dmitri began.

"Yeah?" Lars said.

"He's undercover. You know, KGB, Secret Service? He travels with Slava everywhere he goes."

"Even to the bathroom?" Nish had to know.

"Practically — they're worried about the Russian mob."

"Somebody wants to *kill* your cousin?" Travis asked. He couldn't believe it.

"Not *kill* him, stupid — *kidnap* him!"

"*Kidnap* him?" the other three said at once.

"Yeah, hold him for ransom. You know."

"He's that rich?" Nish asked. He was incredulous.

Dmitri shook his head. "Not rich. He's that *good*."

"Explain," Nish demanded.

"The mob has already blackmailed lots of NHL players. They threaten to harm family members back in Russia and the player pays up. It's simple."

"That's crazy!" Lars said.

"Russia's crazy right now," said Dmitri. "They know what everyone is saying about Slava. They say he's the best ever, as good as Larionov, as good as Fedorov, Bure, Yashin."

"But he has no money," pointed out Travis. "He can't even be drafted until he's eighteen."

"Doesn't matter," said Dmitri. "He means everything to Russian hockey right now. He's the proof that there are still great players coming up through the system. The Russian Ice Hockey Federation only exists because of the money they're getting from NHL teams right now. They'd pay whatever ransom was necessary."

"So they send him over here with bodyguards?" Lars said.

"That's it."

"Ridiculous," Lars said, shaking his head.

Travis had to agree. A thirteen-year-old peewee hockey player? How good could he be?

6

SLAVA SHADRIN'S CSKA TEAM, IN UNIFORMS AS red as the arena seats, was already on the Globen rink when the Screech Owls came out. It took Travis a while to locate number 13. Slava was certainly an elegant skater, but was he better than Sarah Cuthbertson? Travis looked for Sarah and found her circling about the huge ice surface like milkweed floating on a breeze.

Travis hit the crossbar on his first practice shot and knew he was going to have a good game. As team captain, he lined up the Owls to take practice shots at Jennie Staples and Jeremy Weathers. Jennie was getting the first start in the tournament, and she was nervous. More shots were going in than she was keeping out.

Travis's legs felt good. They had been a bit rubbery after the long flight and then the Swedish-style practice, but now everything was back. He moved without effort, quick, fluid, and smooth. He hoped he looked good to the Russians. He hoped they'd noticed his C for "Captain"; he had already noticed the K for "Kaptain" on number 13.

Muck called them all over to the bench. This was most unusual for Muck, who usually spoke only in the dressing room.

"You're here to *play*, not *watch*," Muck said. "Don't let what you see hypnotize you out there. You want number 13's autograph, you can line up and get it when the game's over."

Travis thought Muck was going too far. Slava didn't seem that special. Sarah could skate as well, and Andy Higgins could shoot a puck as hard as any thirteen-year-old Travis had ever seen. He himself was a pretty good playmaker, wasn't he? And who was faster than Dmitri on a break?

"Sarah, he's your check right through the neutral zone," Muck said. "He crosses our blue-line, Nishikawa, and he's all yours. I want you to stick to him like Krazy Glue, both of you. Understand?"

No one said anything. No one had to. Travis hammered his stick on the ice and the others followed suit and then broke from the bench to tap Jennie's pads and get the game under way.

Sarah's line would start. Nish and Data were on defence. Travis felt a little uneasy being back on left wing, but he knew they would play better with Sarah's speed at the middle position. And besides, Sarah had to stick with Slava, who was starting centre for CSKA.

The two teams exchanged gifts – small Canadian flags for the Russians, CSKA pins for the

Canadians – and after they had dropped them off into a pillowcase Mr. Dillinger was holding out from the bench, they skated out to start.

Sarah won the face-off cleanly, knocking the puck on her backhand towards Travis. Travis picked it up, spun back, and dropped the puck to Nish, who looked up and decided to hit Sarah as she broke to split the Russian defence. It was a set play, one they had worked on in practice, and it had gone beautifully before – a quick attack before anyone realized the game had even started.

Nish passed, but the puck slammed straight into a pair of shin pads that seemed to arrive out of nowhere. It was number 13, *Slava*! Two strides and he had left Sarah flying in the other direction – Sarah, who had been supposed to stick to him like Krazy Glue in the neutral zone.

Slava Shadrin split the Owls' defence and flew in on Jennie so fast that the unbelievable happened. Jennie first skated quickly out to cut down the angle, and then, realizing he was simply going to blow by her, she caught and tried to switch instantly into reverse. The move was too sudden and she fell over backwards, flat on her back.

Slava Shadrin went in around the fallen goal-tender, spun in a circle, and dropped the puck between his own legs and into the empty net.

CSKA 1, Screech Owls 0.

Sarah's line knew they were going off even though they'd been on for only eight seconds. They skated off, heads down, and Nish and Data followed.

Muck tapped Andy Higgins on the shoulder. "Tell Jennie to come over here," he said.

Travis looked up, puzzled. Was Muck going to pull her?

Andy's line went out and Jennie skated over to the bench. She was crying.

Muck spoke to her. "Sarah missed her check. Nishikawa missed his check. You were the only one in position. So forget it even happened, okay?"

Muck paused a second, and came as close to smiling as he ever did while working the bench.

"And one more thing," he said. "No matter what happens, you're our goaltender today."

Jennie couldn't speak. By now, everyone knew she had been crying, but no one thought it was funny. She nodded, her mask exaggerating the movement, and turned and skated quickly back to her net. Travis could tell from the way Jennie slammed her stick against the posts and set that she was right back in the game.

Sarah's line didn't get another shift until the second half of the first period, and by then Travis had had every opportunity to see why Slava Shadrin was considered so special.

He had never seen anyone – not even Sarah – skate like that. Slava didn't look particularly fast, his legs didn't pump very quickly, but he moved about the ice so cleverly that he always seemed to appear where he shouldn't be. He was as quick going to both sides as ahead, as fast back-checking as attacking.

When Slava was out there, CSKA always seemed to have the puck. He didn't keep it for himself; he could have it just for a moment – a moment in which it seemed every one of the Owls was turning to check him – and then it would be gone. His passes were like darts, quick little flicks that snapped the puck onto his team-mates' blades, and they would no sooner have the puck than, instantly, Slava was in a wide-open stretch of ice calling for it.

The Russians were up 3–0 when Sarah's line was given another chance. This time she was ready. Wherever Slava went, she went too. She dived to block passes, she stuck to him like a shadow, and Slava seemed to enjoy it.

Once, Slava came in on Nish and stopped so fast that ice chips flew into his face as if they'd been thrown from a snowblower. Slava let the puck slip on under its own momentum and right through Nish's skates. One quick turn and he was once again home free. He cut across the net, getting Jennie to follow, and then slipped a pass back to his winger, who knew exactly what to expect.

CSKA 4, Screech Owls 0.

The Owls found themselves a bit in the second. Sarah knocked a pass from Slava out of the air and hit Travis as he broke up the boards. With the Russian defenceman squeezing him out, Travis remembered what Muck always preached: A shot at the net is never a bad decision. The goaltender let a fat rebound come off right onto the stick of Dmitri, who roofed the puck on his backhand.

CSKA nearly scored again when Slava put a pass back through his legs to the point and the biggest Russian defenceman wound up for a mighty slapshot. Travis knew if he dived he might block the shot, or at least tip it up and away, but he couldn't make himself do it. He stuck out his stick warily and the shot screamed right through and clanged off the crossbar. Lucky for Travis.

Next shift, Muck kept Travis on the bench. Muck was letting him know that he had seen him back off. Travis was still afraid of getting hit with a shot.

As he sat out the shift, Travis glanced up into the crowd. Annika and some of the Malmö team were there, singing and waving their club banner, and, every once in a while, shouting "EEEE-AWWW-KEEE!" when Nish had the puck.

A man was standing beside the Owls' bench. There was something about the cut of his suit and the look of him that told Travis he was another Russian. The man was chewing on a toothpick, and when he worked his lips Travis could see the flash of a gold tooth. He looked nasty. But Travis supposed that was how a Russian undercover cop would look.

Late in the game, Sarah scored on a beautiful solo rush when she split the defence, and big Andy Higgins scored on a shot that went in off the toe of one of the CSKA defence. But they couldn't come all the way back.

The horn sounded and the first game of the tournament was over. CSKA had beaten the Screech Owls 6–3, but it could have been much worse. Jennie Staples had made so many great stops after the first disaster that she was named Canadian Player of the Game. Jennie and Slava Shadrin, the obvious Russian Player of the Game, both received tournament banners.

They lined up and shook hands. Travis was in front of Nish, who was still complaining about one of the goals. Nish hadn't had a great game. Travis came to Slava, who had his hand out and was smiling, his big teeth protruding slightly.

"Good game, captain," Slava said.

"You, too," said Travis. He felt a thrill that such a good player would even notice him out there. And he had noticed Travis's C, as well!

Slava passed on to Nish, who had his hand out but without much enthusiasm. Slava took it, pumped it, and made a kissing sound with his lips.

"*Get a life!*" Nish growled.

7

TRAVIS WOKE WITH A START. HE'D BEEN DREAM-
ing about the man with the gold tooth. The man
had a gun and was chasing them. They were in a
rink, Travis and Nish, and they were in bare feet,
and the man was on skates. And he was raising his
gun to fire . . .

There was light streaming from the bathroom. Four of them were sleeping in the room,
and on his left Travis could see the mound that
was Data, and beyond Data, with the sheets
kicked off and lying flat on his stomach, was Lars.
So it had to be Nish in the bathroom. Travis
waited, but there was no sound. No water
running. Nothing. He remembered Nish had
gone down to the little mall in the evening. He
had said he had to get to a drug store. Maybe he's
not feeling well, Travis thought. Maybe I'd better
check on him.

He rolled out of bed. The sheets stuck to his
back. He'd been sweating. Frightened.

"You okay, Nish?" Travis called lightly.

"Fine," the answer came back, sharply. The
door slammed shut.

Travis waited a while longer. Lars was stirring now and starting to get up. They would be leaving for Malmö at nine, so everyone had to get up and pack. They would need the bathroom.

Travis got up and went to the door, Lars — scratching his sides — right behind him.

"Can we come in?" Travis called.

"*In a minute!*"

Lars yawned. "He's in a good mood this morning."

"I don't think he's feeling well."

They waited a moment longer. Travis tapped his knuckles lightly on the door.

"*Okay, okay, okay!*" Nish called from inside.

They could hear him fiddling with the lock. The door opened — and someone they had never seen before was standing in front of them!

All they could see was the hair. Dark hair, standing almost straight up. Hair moulded into shiny, black spikes. Like stalagmites in a dark cavern. Still dripping with something oily.

"*Nish?*" Lars said.

Below the shining, black spikes, a big Nish grin spread across a vaguely familiar face.

"How do you like it? Just like Borje Salming, don't you think? A little mousse, a little Swedish gel — cost me less than thirty krona."

Travis didn't know what to say. His hair was, well, *bizarre*. It was a *bit* like Borje Salming's, but this was also something entirely unique.

"Well?" Nish demanded.

Lars pushed by, giggling. He elbowed Nish out, closed the door, and locked it. He had to use the facilities.

"*Well?*" Nish said again.

Travis still didn't know what to say. He swallowed hard.

"I think you look like an idiot."

"You're just jealous," Nish said, pushing Travis out of the way so he could dress.

●

Nish's new hair was the highlight of the trip to Malmö. Sarah laughed so hard she had tears rolling down her cheeks. Wilson and Data stood behind his seat holding their noses, for Nish's slicked head had a certain distinctive smell.

"We'll have to drill holes in the top of his helmet," said Muck, shaking his head.

They set off by double-decker tour bus on a cold March morning, but in sunshine so bright it soon heated up the vehicle. Some of the seats were positioned around little card tables with special holders built in for drinks, so the players drank Cokes and played hearts.

They drove south along the coastline and then cut inland, travelling on good, clear highways across the frozen south of Sweden. Travis took off his Screech Owls jacket and stuffed it against his window, then turned and stared out. The bus rolled through countryside with more frozen lakes than Travis had ever seen. On some of the lakes people were ice fishing. There were cars out on the ice, and along the shore Travis saw several saunas – some with smoke rising from them. Once, he could swear he saw a naked man and woman and child rolling in the snow beside one of them, but he didn't say anything.

He didn't want Nish ordering the bus around for a photo opportunity.

"EEEE–AWWW–KEEE!"

Nish was up at the front of the bus even before it passed the Malmö train station on the way to their hotel. They turned left, then right, and finally down a street so narrow it seemed the bus would scrape along both sides until it got stuck. They were at the Master Johan Hotel, their home for the next four nights.

"*Sit down, Nishikawa!*" Muck ordered from his seat just behind the driver.

But it was no use. Nish was already down the stairwell and at the door. Outside, running to catch up, were several Malmö kids, Annika in the lead.

"EEEE–AWWW–KEEE!" Annika shouted.

"*Nish has found his true love!*" Lars called. Everyone laughed.

The Owls spilled off the bus. They were stiff and tired. Sarah and Dmitri were jogging on the spot, trying to loosen up. Nish was high-fiving Annika and her friends and acting as if he were some visiting ambassador.

"Gillar du hans hår?" ("How do you like his hair?") Lars asked Annika.

"Häftigt!" ("Awesome!")

The Malmö team had already beaten the team from Germany and they were all planning to attend the Screech Owls' game against Finland.

"We're going to cheer for Canada," Annika told Nish.

Canada? Travis hadn't thought of it that way before. To him, they were the Screech Owls. But to these kids, they were Team Canada – just as Kariya and Gretzky and even Paul Henderson had played for Team Canada. They were representing their *country*. Travis felt a tremendous glow of pride come over him. And responsibility.

He was *captain* of the Canadian team.

8

THE MASTER JOHAN WAS PERFECT. THE ROOMS were huge, with cots thrown in so there could be four or five players per room. It was the fanciest hotel Travis and most of the other Owls had ever stayed at – marble sinks, deep carpets, and a huge courtyard under a glass roof where they served breakfast.

They slept well – no nightmares for Travis this time – and in the morning were given time off to do anything they wanted. Most of the parents were going shopping or to the art museum. A few of the mothers were even going to take the hovercraft across the sound to Copenhagen, in Denmark, for a day of shopping. Heading across the sea to another country seemed no more unusual to the people of Malmö than getting in the van to drive down to the mall.

"There's a castle about five minutes from here," Mr. Johanssen told the kids.

"A castle!" Data screeched.

Mr. Johanssen laughed. "You're in Europe, young man. There are castles everywhere. This one is more than five hundred years old – and it used to be a prison."

"Did they torture people there?"

"I don't know, but some prisoners were executed," Mr. Johanssen said. "But that was a long, long time ago."

"Let's go! Let's go!" shouted Data.

But not everyone wanted to go. Several of the Owls were headed off shopping with their parents. Nish insisted on going to McDonald's with Annika and her friends. In the end about a half-dozen of the Owls went with Mr. Johanssen to see Malmöhus Castle. Data, of course, and Wilson, Andy, Travis, Dmitri, and Lars.

The castle wasn't at all like the one at the entrance to Disney World's Magic Kingdom, but it did have an old moat, and two gun towers were still standing, and it *felt* very old. Travis ran two rolls of film through his camera.

Mr. Johanssen and Lars led them on a tour. What they couldn't see they had to imagine. The castle had also been used as a mint for making coins, as a home for the poor, as a prison – and even as an asylum.

Now it was used for various exhibitions, usually art, but this month featured a special display, "Arms and Armour: Norse and Viking Warriors." They passed through room after room of shiny metal armour, chain mail, shields, swords, spiked flails, mace, and spears.

"Hollywood got it all wrong in the Viking movies," Mr. Johanssen told them. "The basic Viking weapon was the *spear*, not the sword."

But the most fascinating display was the room filled with helmets, some of them real, some of them replicas that they were allowed to touch. There were cone-shaped helmets and helmets that covered all of the head, with only tiny slits to see out through. "Still enough room to stab a sword in," Data pointed out. Travis winced.

"This," said one of the museum guards, picking up a replica of a beautifully curved helmet with stems running down over each ear and another to protect the nose, "is a *spangenhelm*. It's what a Viking warrior would wear."

He turned to Travis, smiling. "You want to try it on?"

"Me?" Travis asked.

"Sure, go ahead."

With the others giggling, Travis reached out and took the huge helmet. It weighed about three times what he expected! "Careful now!" the guard laughed. "Don't drop it!"

With the guard's help, Travis pulled the helmet over his head. He could barely keep his neck straight. He couldn't believe that anyone could even walk with something like this on, let alone head into battle!

"How'd you like to play hockey in something like that?" Mr. Johanssen asked.

"No way!" said Travis.

They helped him off with the helmet, placed it back on the display shelf, and moved into another area with even more weapons.

"Where did they execute the prisoners?" Data asked.

"I can show you," Mr. Johanssen said, smiling, and he led them out to the courtyard.

"I'm going to tell you about something that happened right here at this spot on September 19, 1837," Mr. Johanssen began. Travis tried to imagine how long ago that was.

"The prison governor at the time, Hans Canon, was a hard, cruel man. He used to have his prisoners flogged for the slightest reason."

"What's flogged?" Wilson asked.

"Whipped. Their shirts stripped off and their backs beaten with leather straps until their skin peeled away. Sometimes they bled to death."

"Awesome," said Data.

"You're a mental case," said Travis.

Mr. Johanssen continued. "There were two particularly evil criminals here then. Karlqvist and Wahlgren. The governor hated them both, but particularly Karlqvist, who wore his hair long and was a bit of a loudmouth. One day the governor got so fed up with Karlqvist's behaviour that he came out here and had him dragged inside, and when he had been strapped to a chair, the governor himself cut his hair.

"I guess he did a pretty awful job, because they threw Karlqvist back out here in the courtyard and all the other prisoners laughed at him. But Governor Canon made the mistake of coming out to gloat. Wahlgren and his friend had knives, and the two of them attacked the governor right here where you're standing."

Travis looked down at the rough bricks. The image of the two men stabbing at the governor flashed through his mind. He shivered.

"Was there blood?" Data asked.

Mr. Johanssen laughed — once, and very quickly. "A lot of blood. The governor died of his wounds."

"What happened to the two men?" Andy asked.

"They cut their heads off."

"Here?" Data asked.

"Right here."

"Right off?"

"Right off."

Data looked at the ground as if the bricks still ran red with blood. He stepped away carefully, almost afraid he'd trip on a rolling, bloody head.

"All because of somebody's *hair*?" Data asked.

"All because of somebody's hair," Mr. Johanssen said. "Nish is lucky he's living today and not back then."

9

THE MALMÖ ICE STADIUM WAS MUCH MORE like a regular Canadian hockey rink than was the strange Globen "golf ball" in Stockholm. At the snack bar, the Owls, who were used to seeing a pop machine at best, couldn't get over the fact that they were selling ice cream and that parents and older players were lining up to buy beer.

The Owls were to face the Finnish team from Tampere. The Finns had already beaten one of the Swedish teams and were said to be almost as good as the Russians. This time, however, it wasn't the way the opposition skated and shot that impressed the Owls during warmup – it was their advertising.

The Tampere team had blue jerseys and socks and red pants, but the blue of their jerseys was almost hidden under the ads for car oil, computers, stereo systems, even a bank.

"They're gonna be slowed down by all the advertising," said Data as he and Travis circled at the blueline, warily watching the Tampere players as they took shots.

Travis laughed. But perhaps Data was right. They didn't seem as swift as the Russians. Certainly, none skated like Slava Shadrin.

The Malmö rink itself was one big commercial. There wasn't a board without advertising. Banners hung from the low ceiling, promoting SAS airlines, Volvo, Burger King . . .

"When we get back home, I'm selling *my* body, too."

Travis turned, surprised. It was Nish.

"Whatdya mean?" Travis asked.

"I'm renting out my uniform. McDonald's, Nintendo, Nike – you name it, I'm going for it."

"They'd never let you."

"What's it to them? Maybe a big 'Coke' painted on the top of my helmet. Whatdya say?"

"You're nuts."

Just as the warmup was about to end, Travis effortlessly deked Jeremy out of the net and backhanded a shot off the crossbar. He could hear his teammates cheer. Funny, he thought. In a game, goals count; in practice and in warmups, crossbars are what matter. He had his crossbar. He was certain to play well.

The Finns had tremendous puck control. They seemed to work the larger ice surface better, especially the defence, but even though the team from Tampere had the puck more, the Owls seemed to know better what to do with it. Andy

Higgins scored on a hard shot through a screen, but the Finns tied the game late in the first period after Nish had got caught badly out of position.

At the break, Travis took a look at the crowd as the Owls headed off to their dressing room. He knew Annika was there – she'd been doing that stupid yell every time Nish touched the puck – but he hadn't seen Slava's team come in. The Russians were just taking their seats behind the Owls' bench, all with dull-red team jackets, all sitting down as if they were getting ready for a class. They probably were, Travis thought; they were here to study the opposition.

Sitting just behind Slava were the two men they had seen at the Russian team's dressing room. They seemed strategically placed, watching. The man with the gold tooth wasn't there.

Muck didn't seem particularly pleased with the 1–1 score.

"Nishikawa," he began, "would you mind explaining what 'cycling' is?"

Nish didn't look up. He sat doubled over on the wooden bench with his folded arms pressed between his chest and knees. He stared at the floor as he answered.

"All three forwards work the puck in the same corner. Each one drops the puck back as he circles and then blocks the checker. If there's a clear opening, the player picking up the puck walks out for the shot."

"And did you see that out there today?"

"Yes."

"And did it work?"

"Yes."

"It worked because you fell for the lure. If you don't bite, they can't block you. And if they can't block you, they can't come out."

"I thought I had a play."

"That's the idea, isn't it? You thought you did and you didn't. And they scored on us because you fell for it."

Nish said nothing. He knew.

Muck had only a few words for the rest of them.

"We're here to play hockey, not sightsee. You want to take pictures, you do it out of uniform, okay?"

The second period saw a dramatic change. It was not just the way the game was played, it was also the sound level. Annika's calls for Nish were now all but drowned out by the whistling and shouting, and once even a song, from the Russians sitting behind the Owls' bench.

"How come they're cheering for us?" Travis asked Dmitri when they were off for a shift.

Dmitri smiled. "I thought they were cheering for *me*."

This time Nish let the Finns cycle all they wanted. He maintained his position and simply stepped into any player who dared come out of the corners with the puck to try him one-on-one. If he saw a chance to go for the puck, he took the player and left the puck for the forward coming back. The Finns never got another good scoring chance.

Sarah gave the Owls the lead with a beautiful two-on-one with Dmitri. She let Dmitri break for the net, but, instead of passing to him, she slowed and cut across the slot. The one defenceman who had been in position simply drifted out of the play with Dmitri, and the goalie had to move with Sarah. Once she had him going the wrong way, she slid a hard backhand along the ice that ticked in off the far post.

The Finns pulled their goalie in the final minute. Travis tried to block a shot at the point, but didn't drop down in time. It didn't matter, as the shot went high and wide, but Travis knew he had hesitated. It had looked as if he'd tried his best, but he hadn't. He'd paused, and even when he did go down he'd kept his eyes closed, afraid of the puck.

Lars ended the tension when he scored in the empty Finnish net with a long shot that barely had enough weight to carry it over the goal line.

The Owls were 1–1 for the tournament.

They still had a chance.

10

THE TELEPHONE RANG IN THE BOYS' ROOM AT
the Master Johan. Nish, who had been trying,
once again, to unscramble the television so they
could watch free adult movies – "Sweden
invented sex!" he'd shouted – threw down the
loose wires in disgust and rolled across the bed to
scoop up the phone.

"*What?*" he demanded. His rewiring was not
working out. He was getting frustrated.

Nish held the phone out towards Travis.

"It's for you."

"Who is it?"

"Whatdya think I am, your secretary?"

It was Dmitri. He wanted to meet Travis
immediately by the elevator on the fifth floor. He
couldn't explain. He wanted Travis to bring Nish
and Lars but wouldn't say why.

Nish agreed to go only reluctantly. He was
close, he said, to cracking the problem. Travis
looked at the back of the television. Loose wires
were everywhere. He only hoped Nish would be
able to put it all back together again.

Dmitri was waiting for them at the elevator. "Slava called me," he said. "He wants to go out with us."

"Fine," said Travis. "Where are we going?"

"To McDonald's — he just wants to get away."

"So why the secret meeting?" Nish demanded.

"They won't let him go anywhere. Those two bodyguards watch him like a hawk."

"I thought there were three," said Travis.

Dmitri blinked at Travis. "He says two."

"But I've seen a third," Travis said, thinking of the man with the gold tooth.

"Two, three, whatever. He just wants to hang out. He wants us to bring along Sarah, if we can."

"I've got a date with Annika," Nish said.

"A *date*?" Lars asked.

"Okay, I'm supposed to get together with her."

"Where?"

"Same place — McDonald's. A little later."

"So we'll all be there together," said Dmitri.

"Call Slava," Travis said.

"It's not that simple," Dmitri said. "We have to break him out of here."

"*What?*"

"They won't let him go. He's got no life apart from playing hockey."

"Hockey *is* life," said Nish.

"He just wants to be a kid," said Dmitri. "Lars, you've got to phone and get one of the bodyguards to go down to the front desk. Slava says he can give the other the slip."

"Won't he get in trouble?" Lars asked.

"Muck would sit one of us out if we did anything like that," Travis said.

Dmitri shook his head. "You don't understand. Slava is the best player in Russia. *He* won't get in any trouble. *They* will."

"Who will?"

"The guys guarding him."

Lars went to one of the house phones and Dmitri dialled the number and handed the receiver over to him. The boys heard a click, then a man's muffled voice. Lars spoke quickly, in Swedish. The man obviously understood. Lars had lowered his voice, and though the boys couldn't understand what he was saying, he sounded very authoritative. The man seemed to be shouting back, angrily. Lars spoke again, very calmly, and hung up.

"Did it work?" Dmitri asked.

"I think so. He should be headed down to the front desk."

"What did you tell him?" Travis asked.

"Nish gave me the idea," Lars smiled. "I told him his players had been fooling with the television sets. I said he was going to be charged 340 krona for the movies they had watched. He got mad and I told him if he wished to discuss the matter he'd have to meet with the manager."

"Brilliant!" Dmitri said, snapping his fingers.

They called Sarah's room next. She was delighted to be asked along. They ran into Data and tried to get him to come, too, but he said he thought he was getting a bad cold and didn't want to go out.

"*Gimme a second!*" Nish shouted at the last moment. He raced up to his room, reappearing a couple of minutes later at the elevator doors. His hair was freshly moussed and gelled and shining, smelling like room refreshener.

They met Sarah in the lobby and all went outside, skirting around to the street behind the Master Johan, where they had arranged to wait for Slava. Several minutes passed, and they had all but lost hope, when the rear door to the hotel opened and a slim young man in a red jacket slipped out, his cap pulled down tight over his eyes.

It was Slava. He ran over, shouting to Dmitri as he reached his new friends.

Dmitri laughed. "He locked the other guy in the washroom by jamming a hockey stick under the handle!"

Slava was now shaking hands with Sarah — very formal for a bunch of kids from North

America. Sarah giggled; yet she seemed flattered, charmed by Slava's old-world ways.

"Let's get going!" Nish said.

They headed up towards McDonald's. It was a dull early-spring day, the clouds so low they spread like a thick grey blanket over the city.

At the first corner there were streetlights and a small bridge over a narrow canal which led towards the park where the old castle stood. It was quiet, with little traffic, and they began to relax a bit as they headed over the bridge.

"EEEE-AWWW-KEEE!" Nish shouted. There was no response. Annika wasn't within range.

Travis didn't feel quite right, but the others seemed at ease. Slava and Sarah were walking together, but saying nothing. Nish was calling out constantly. If he was this bad now, what would he be like when they got to McDonald's?

Travis began to feel something was really wrong. At the far end of the bridge, a car had come to a stop. It must have slid on some ice, for it had swung sideways and was blocking their path. Two men were getting out.

Travis looked back to see if any traffic was coming towards them from the other end of the bridge. A dark van had slid the same way on that side, too! Another man was getting out.

It was the man with the gold tooth!

"*Watch out!*" Travis shouted.

But already it was too late. The others had noticed as well, and were ready to run – but they were trapped. The car blocked one end of the bridge; the van the other.

The quickest way off the bridge was to head back and take their chances with the man with the gold tooth, but as Lars and Travis started to move that way, they saw the man reach into his coat.

He had a gun!

"*Run for it!*" said Dmitri. "*It's them!*"

No one had to explain who. *The Russian mob was making its move!*

The five friends turned, scrambling frantically, not knowing which way to run. Travis caught sight of Nish's face: beet red, terrified.

The other two men were now running towards them.

"*They're after Slava!*" shouted Dmitri. "*We can't let him go!*"

"*Grab onto him!*" shouted Sarah.

She threw her arms around Slava just as the first two men reached them. One of the men roughly grabbed Slava by the arm and yanked – but now Dmitri also had a hold of his cousin and was desperately hanging on. The man yanked again, harder.

Travis had to do something! He was afraid, but he had to act. He dived for Slava's legs and caught him in a perfect tackle.

"HANG ON!" Dmitri screamed.

A boot lashed out and caught Travis on the side of the head. He saw a blinding flash of light, almost as if lightning had struck from inside his head. The pain was incredible, but still he held on. He was not going to chicken out!

Travis felt a huge weight come down on him. Out of his uninjured eye he could see it was Nish. His friend had leapt into action, too, but instead of going for Slava's legs, he had tackled the foot that had kicked Travis! It was the man with the gold tooth! The man went down hard on the roadway of the bridge, his gun spilling away.

KA-BOOOOOOM!

The stunning crack of the gun was followed by instant, eerie silence. Everyone lay still a moment. No one moved.

Travis looked up. The man with the gold tooth had hold of his gun again and was pointing it at them and shaking it. He was very upset.

"Get up!" he barked out in Russian.

"Everybody just get up slowly!" Dmitri translated.

The Owls rose slowly. Travis's head was screaming. He thought he was going to be sick. *Was he going to be shot? Were they going to kill Slava?*

"Move!"

"We're all to get in the van," Dmitri said.

Everybody? Why everybody? Travis wondered. But he also knew this was no time for him to raise his hand to ask a question. This wasn't a classroom.

The men hurried the friends towards the van at the near end of the bridge. Travis listened for police sirens. Someone must have heard the shot.

The men opened the rear doors of the van and roughly shoved their captives inside. Travis struck his head again, this time on Nish's knee.

He felt sick to his stomach. The van smelled of bad cigarettes. He could smell Nish's hair.

Sarah was shoved in on top of him, then Slava and Dmitri. Travis managed to sit up and caught sight of Slava.

He was white as a ghost.

"Move it!" the man with the gold tooth shouted in Russian.

The van wheels spun in the light snow, the rear end fishtailing as it turned on the quiet road and sped away in the opposite direction. The Russians were abandoning the car at the far end of the bridge, where it was still blocking the roadway.

Gold Tooth turned and swatted at them.

"Get down!" he shouted.

"Duck down!" Dmitri translated. He pushed Slava and Sarah down over the other two.

A heavy blanket flew over from the front seat, covering them.

The blinding flashes in Travis's head gave way to darkness.

11

MUCK AND MR. DILLINGER WERE WAITING FOR the elevator in the lobby of the Master Johan, but when the doors slid open, they were almost trampled by the CSKA coach and the two body-guards coming out. The coach looked furious, the bodyguards upset. They didn't even nod hello.

Mr. Dillinger, his eyes wide, turned to Muck. "What's got into them, I wonder?"

But before Muck could answer, there was more activity. The doors leading from the lobby to the street swung open and Mr. Johanssen hurried in with a concerned look on his face. The sound of a police siren outside filled the lobby momentarily.

"There's been a shot!" Mr. Johanssen called out to the man at the front desk as he walked, fast, towards the elevators.

"*What's going on?*" Mr. Dillinger called to Mr. Johanssen.

"There's been a report of a gun fired behind the hotel."

Muck turned back towards the elevators. "I better check on the team."

Travis thought he could hear a dog bark. There were also sirens in the distance. Sirens were different in Sweden – almost as if they were breathing in and out quickly – but they were definitely sirens. Police, he hoped. Someone must have heard the gun go off.

Travis couldn't tell how long they'd been gone. An hour? Two? Muck would be wondering where they were. And the Russians would have panicked once they found out Slava had given them the slip. Even Data would have wondered what was taking so long with his fries.

Travis had no idea where he was. He had been unable to see anything from the back of the van, and the men had kept the blanket over their heads as they pushed and shoved them into wherever they were now. He could smell smoke, something burning. He was lying on his side and could barely see. His right eye was swollen almost shut.

The floor was very hard. Harder even than wood. And cold. There was a smell in the air, almost musty, something like the backyard in spring when the snow melts away and his mother would turn over the garden. The air felt cool, and damp, and cellar-like.

Travis wanted to roll over, but he couldn't. His hands were tied behind his back. He shook off the blanket that had been tossed over him and blinked in the darkness. There was a light somewhere behind him, a light flickering on the wall. He thought he could make out the patterns of stone. A stone wall. He was cold, and shivering.

He painfully sat upright. He could see Sarah sitting the same way, but with her back to the stone wall. Dmitri and Slava were also sitting with their hands tied behind them, and he caught Dmitri's eye. Dmitri was silently urging him to stay quiet; he jerked his head slightly, indicating something behind Travis.

Slowly, Travis twisted around. He saw Nish against the wall. He had his eyes closed and was shaking, but whether he was crying quietly or shivering from the cold, Travis couldn't tell.

He was able to turn his head far enough to see what Dmitri was signalling. Two of their captors – one of them the man with the gold tooth – were in the room with them. They were both smoking, but that wasn't what Travis had smelled. They were huddled close to a small naphtha heater. It was a camping heater, like Travis's father had. It was giving off some warmth, but not nearly enough to take the chill out of the room. The heater was what he had smelled.

The two men were speaking, very low, in Russian. One seemed angry, and also anxious.

Travis was surprised to hear Dmitri whisper, "Keep it low. Those two don't understand English."

Travis turned back. "Do you think they're really the mob?"

"I guess so. We knew they wanted Slava – they just didn't expect to end up with us, too."

Nish was now looking up. His whisper was a hiss, a bit too loud, and filled with fear. "*Where are we?*"

One of the men yelled at him to shut up.

The men were talking very fast now, their anger rising. Dmitri and Slava watched and listened, and Travis watched Dmitri, trying to read his expression. As Dmitri listened he seemed to grow more and more worried.

Travis decided to risk a whisper: "*What are they fighting about?*"

Dmitri blinked: "*Us.*"

"*Whadya mean?*" Nish hissed.

"*Shhhhhh . . .*"

Gold Tooth stood up from the small heater and kicked angrily at a blanket that caught his foot. He turned and glared at the kids. Travis had never seen such hatred in anyone's eyes. He shivered – and not, this time, from the cold.

Gold Tooth then suddenly stormed out, lifting a solid wooden plank that was blocking the old door, and slamming it as he left.

The second man looked up sharply at the slam and then went back to eating the bread and cheese that he had pulled out of a sack. He also had beer, and when he opened one of the bottles the smell of it drifted across the dank room.

For a long time no one dared say anything. The man ate and grumbled to himself and threw a blanket around his shoulders. He opened another beer, then filled the little heater with naphtha and lighted it again, turning it up high.

Dmitri suddenly spoke up in Russian: "Can you please hang one of these blankets over that window? We're freezing!"

"Shut up!" the man snapped. He fiddled some more with the heater, then looked back at Dmitri with an evil smile. Dmitri had given him an idea.

The man gathered several of the old blankets. One he strung across the window, catching it on a nail on either side.

"Thank God," whispered Sarah.

But the man was thinking only of himself. He pulled his heater over into a corner of the room and assembled a sort of rough tent out of blankets strung across a chair and a stool and an old storage box. He moved the heater inside, then his beer. With one more sly smile at the shivering kids, he ducked down into his private, cosy little shelter.

"*Thanks a lot!*" Nish hissed with great sarcasm.

"I'm freezing!" said Sarah.

"No!" said Travis. "We want this!"

"We *want* to freeze to death?" Nish asked.

Travis hurried to explain. "My dad says never take one of those heaters inside a tent."

"Why not?" Dmitri asked.

"It gives off carbon monoxide gas."

"So?" Nish said.

"So – he'll kill himself, if he doesn't kill us first."

"We're being poisoned?" Sarah asked.

"Not us," said Travis. "There's too much fresh air getting in here through the cracks. But he's blocking himself off."

"What was the big fight over?" Lars asked Dmitri.

Dmitri didn't seem to want to say. "They were just arguing."

"What did they say?"

"Nothing."

Travis knew Dmitri was keeping something from them. "You'd better tell us," he said.

Dmitri swallowed hard and looked at Slava. His cousin couldn't understand much English, but Slava seemed to know what they were discussing anyway. He looked scared.

"The guy who left doesn't want the rest of us around," Dmitri said finally.

Nish brightened up. "They're going to let us go?"

"I'm not sure that's what he had in mind."

Dmitri would say no more, but Travis's imagination filled the rest in: they would be shot, or they would be left here to starve . . .

Travis's head and eye began to throb, badly.

Panic was setting in at the Master Johan. The parents and coaches and the rest of the Screech Owls were gathered in the lobby, but instead of calming each other down, the players were feeding off each other's fears. They were imagining every possible disaster that could befall their missing friends – even murder.

"The police are searching the city," Mr. Johanssen told them after a man in uniform had come in and talked to him. "There's no way anyone could get out of Malmö with all those youngsters and not get caught. They put up roadblocks immediately.

"Has there been a call?" asked Muck.

"One. Just to say they have Slava."

"What about the Screech Owls?"

Mr. Johanssen swallowed hard. "We have to presume," he said, "that they're with Slava."

Muck got up and walked to the window,

staring out at a city he didn't know. He had never felt so helpless in his life.

The captives had no idea where Gold Tooth had gone. Probably he was making a call about the ransom.

"I'm so hungry I could eat blood pudding," Nish said.

Travis couldn't help himself: he giggled.

Another empty beer bottle dropped and rolled along the floor, and Travis heard the man burp. His breathing was becoming loud and uneven. The man was falling asleep. All that beer and the carbon monoxide was getting to him.

"*He's passing out!*" Travis whispered to the others.

Sarah strained to see past the hanging blankets, but could hardly move with her hands and feet tied.

"*Shhhhhh*," she said. "*Wait!*"

They waited. The man's breathing continued to grow ever slower, deeper. Finally he began to snore.

Sarah twisted over onto her side. In the poor light, Travis could see her twisting and pulling at her bonds. He heard her stifle a cry once. It was no use; she was just hurting herself.

"Nish!" Sarah said quickly. "Get over here!"

Nish blinked. "What for?"

"Just do it! Quick – Gold Tooth could come back any minute!"

Nish groaned but did as he was told. He fell over onto his side and then rolled across the room until he was close to Sarah.

"*I feel like a worm!*" he complained.

"You *are* a worm!" Sarah said. "Now twist your stupid head around here so I can get at it!"

"What?"

"Just do as you're told! And hurry!"

As soon as Nish was within reach, Sarah turned her back to him and began rubbing her bound hands back and forth over his hair.

"*You're hurting me!*" Nish complained.

"Just shut up, Nish!" Sarah said. "I need your grease!"

So that was it! Travis watched as Sarah very deliberately rubbed her wrists back and forth over Nish's heavily greased hair, working in the mousse and gel so the ropes would slide. Back and forth, back and forth, back and forth over Nish's magnificent hairdo.

Nish whimpered almost in silence: "*Ow-ow-ow-ow-ow-ow . . .*"

Sarah worked a little longer, then stopped and caught her breath. "I'm going to try it," she said.

She took a deep breath and pulled as hard as she could. Nothing. She took another deep breath and yanked harder — *and her right hand came out!*

"*I'm free!*"

12

THE MALMÖ POLICE HAD COME TO THE MASTER
Johan with police dogs. They let them sniff some
of the Screech Owls' hockey equipment, but the
dogs had been unable to pick up any trail as the
police worked them around the nearby streets.

Muck was beside himself. It was all his fault,
he told anyone who would listen. He should
never have let them wander about on their own
. . . He should never have let them leave the hotel
without informing him . . . He should have
known that Dmitri would try to get together
with his cousin Slava . . .

Muck clenched his hands into tight fists and
chewed fiercely on his lower lip.

"*Muck?*"

The small voice behind him caught Muck off
guard. It was Data, and he was trembling.

"I think I might have an idea . . ."

Sarah worked quickly. She untied her own feet,
and then moved to untie Travis. He could hear

her breathing. It seemed like she was fighting back tears, and in the dim light Travis could see that one of her wrists was bleeding.

No one said a word. They scrambled to untie the others and then all moved quietly towards the tent made of blankets.

When Travis lifted one corner, he could smell the naphtha and feel the heat inside against his face. The Russian was lying on his back, breathing deep and long and very, very slow. His throat rattled with each long-drawn breath.

"He's out cold!" Lars said.

Travis moved to turn off the heater.

"Leave it!" Nish said. "We haven't time!"

"He could die if we don't get some fresh air to him," Travis said. He turned off the heater and ripped down the blankets so the air from outside would get in.

Sarah was already at work, trussing the man's hands and feet with rope. He never even stirred.

Lars tried the door. It gave a bit. He pulled and it creaked loudly.

"*Shhhhhhhhh!*" Dmitri hissed.

"What should we do?" Travis asked.

"*Run for it!*" said Nish.

"What if Gold Tooth's coming back?" Sarah asked. "He's the one who wants to kill us."

Lars yanked the door the rest of the way open. "I thought so," he said.

"Thought *what*?" said Nish.

"It's the castle!"

Travis looked around. The *castle*? Where they'd come with Lars's father?

"This is the old prison part," Lars said. He seemed very sure of himself, excited. "The courtyard is just across there."

The courtyard: where the two murderers stabbed the warden, and where they lost their heads, for a haircut. Travis couldn't help but think of the dead warden, bleeding to death on the stones.

"There was that armour exhibition," Travis said, not quite so sure. This didn't seem at all the same.

"This is the really old part," said Lars. "The exhibition should be . . . ," he turned in the dark, searching, ". . . up this way."

"Won't they find us?" Sarah asked.

"It's Sunday – I th-think," said Lars, slowly. "It will be closed."

"We've got to head for the courtyard," said Travis.

"You're right," Lars said. "If we get there, we know how to get out."

"*Which way?*" called Nish.

"This way," Lars said, heading down the dark-ened corridor. "I think."

"*You better be sure,*" said Nish. He sounded scared.

It was dark, but not quite pitch black. There

was light leaking in through the occasional window or crack in the walls. Lights from cars passing, perhaps. Or searchlights, Travis hoped. He thought he heard another dog bark. Once, he thought he heard Nish's stupid call.

Then he knew he had heard it: "*Eeee-awww-keee!*" faint and distant.

"*That's Annika!*" Nish hissed.

They stopped and listened. Again the call.

"Hoist me up!" Nish said.

There was a window, with a crack between the sill and frame. Lars and Dmitri and Slava grabbed onto Nish's legs and lifted. He grasped the sill and pulled. When he reached as close as he could, he shouted out.

"EEEE–AWWW–KEEE!"

From the distance, faintly, the call came back. "*Eeee-awww-keee!*"

"I think she heard!" Nish said.

He was about to call again when they heard a mighty creak and clatter of metal from far down the corridor.

"*Shhhhh!*" Lars said. The boys let Nish back down, quickly and quietly.

They could hear footsteps. Heavy shoes. A man, moving quickly.

"*It's Gold Tooth!*" Travis said.

They listened. There were more steps. And then two voices. *Russian* voices. And angry.

"There's *two* of them!" Nish hissed.

"Who's the other?" Sarah gasped.

Dmitri listened to the hurried, angry talk. "It sounds like Gold Tooth's boss. He's really upset. They can't get through to the Russian team. There's police all around the hotel. He's blaming Gold Tooth for involving us in it."

"What do you mean?"

Dmitri paused. "The new guy wants to shoot us and try to get Slava out of here."

"*Why us?*" Nish squealed. "*We're not going to the NHL.*"

"We've *seen* them," Dmitri explained. "We know what they look like."

Nish was silent. He was beginning to realize just how much danger they were in.

"What'll we do?" Sarah asked.

It was Lars who answered. "If they're talking like that, they didn't hear Nish's call. They don't know we're out. We've got surprise on our side."

"*Whatdya mean?*" Nish asked.

Lars seemed very thoughtful, very thorough. "Look, they're going to come through that doorway ahead. Maybe we can latch it shut and cut them off."

"They'll know we did it," cautioned Travis.

"Maybe. Or maybe they'll just think it swung closed. What's it matter anyway? We have to stop them. Gold Tooth's got a gun, remember?"

A sound came out of Nish. Not quite a whimper. More animal than human.

"C'mon!" Lars called to Travis. The two boys hurried ahead to the big door. They pulled together, and with a creak the door gave and swung shut. Travis hoped the men were still talking and wouldn't hear it. Lars set the latch.

"What now?" Sarah asked.

"I don't know," Lars said. He sounded scared. "The door will only block them for a minute."

What could they do? Travis's head was hurting from more than just the blow from Gold Tooth's boot. He was trying to think as fast as he could.

He had an idea! It wasn't like a light bulb going off in his head, but there was almost a flash. He suddenly felt excited. "The display?" he said. "Where is it?"

Lars turned. "Huh?"

"The armour display. How do we get there?"

Lars thought a moment. "I think it's straight back that way."

Travis didn't waste a second. "Nish, come with me?"

"Wh-wh-where?"

"Never mind. C'mon!"

He hurried ahead through the dark, Nish scrambling behind him. They passed by the prison cell where they'd been held and where, they hoped, the Russian was still passed out cold. They came to a modern door. With his heart beating wildly, Travis drove his shoulder hard against the door and almost choked with excitement when it gave slightly. It was enough for two young shoulders to push hard the rest of the way. A cheap latch and padlock ripped out of the wood and dropped harmlessly on the floor.

They were in!

A few lights had been left on for security. Travis hoped they had triggered an alarm at the police station. Whatever brought them here as fast as possible was all right with him. This was no false alarm.

They were not far from the display of Viking spears. "Grab a couple of those!" he commanded Nish.

Nish waded into the display, reaching with shaking hands. The spears jumbled and clattered to the floor like hockey sticks in a dressing room. He scrambled to pick up two.

Travis headed into the next room. He knew exactly what he wanted.

The spangenhelm!

"What *is* that?"

Sarah was looking at Travis in amazement. He had handed her one of the spears. Nish was holding the other. Travis had the big *spangenhelm* on tight over his head. He knew he must look idiotic. He could barely keep his head off his chest it was so heavy. His head was rolling, his neck muscles weakening.

Dmitri and Slava were also armed. Dmitri had a flail, its heavy spiked head dragging on the ground beside him. Slava had a huge iron mace, so heavy he could barely lift the massive club.

"What the heck am I supposed to do with *this*?" Dmitri asked. He seemed very uncertain.

Travis himself was uncertain. He didn't know exactly why he'd collected the armour. But he did know they'd need something – *and fast!*

The Russians had reached the latched door. They could hear the sound of surprise in Gold Tooth's voice when he found that their route to the prison cells had been blocked. There was a rattling of the latch, then banging at the door.

"They're breaking it down," said Sarah.

Travis turned to Dmitri and Slava. "Move ahead and get down in the dark on each side. You guys will have to trip one of them up."

"How?" asked Dmitri.

"Swing your weapons as hard as you can," Travis said.

Dmitri and Slava moved a little closer to the door and ducked down into the shadows.

Travis turned to Nish and Sarah. "They go down, you two have to make sure they stay down," he said.

"Understood," said Sarah.

With a mighty groan and snap, the big door gave. They could hear the Russians cursing and kicking it as they passed. They couldn't tell whether Gold Tooth thought it was an accident or deliberate.

The two men hurried along the corridor towards the young friends, their heavy steps growing closer. Travis peered into the distance. He could see their shadows looming in the darkness as they approached.

The friends kept completely silent, but for the wheeze of Nish's breathing.

Closer . . . Closer . . . Closer . . .

"*Now!*" Travis shouted.

Dmitri and Slava swung their weapons at exactly the same time. Travis and the others could hear the sickly sound of metal against bone, and the screams of the first Russian as he went down.

"EEEEOOOOOOWWWWWW!"

Only one went down! Gold Tooth stumbled, but caught himself on the far wall. He turned, cursing.

Sarah had already moved to set her spear against the neck of the fallen man. Nish was right behind her, his spear shaking.

In the dim light, Travis could see Gold Tooth fumbling in his coat.

He was reaching for his gun!

Travis pulled down the *spangenhelm*, lowered his head, and charged. *Straight for Gold Tooth's gut!*

KAAA-BOOOOOOMMM!!

The gun exploded. The enormous, shocking sound filled the corridor instantly. It filled Travis's head and he felt the helmet jerk, then smash into something soft.

"Oooooohhh!!"

It was the sound of Gold Tooth's breath being forced from his body as Travis drove his head into his stomach. He felt the man's legs give way, and then Travis hit the floor, the heavy helmet ringing as it struck stone.

He had done it.

Travis rose unsteadily to his feet. Gold Tooth gasped again and sank back. The other man was howling, holding his shin and trying to keep away from the spears.

Suddenly the corridor filled with another loud sound. Not a shot, but a voice – a loudspeaker.

"*Stanna där du är! Rör dig inte!*" ("Stay exactly where you are! Don't move!")

Gold Tooth looked up, still fighting for his breath. There was fury in his eyes. There were dogs barking. And men running.

"*Ingen rör sig!*" ("No one move!") a voice commanded over the speaker.

There were lights now. Flashlights in the corridor; searchlights panning across the walls, spilling in through the small windows.

Two police dogs raced into the room, barking, their handlers right behind them.

One dog leapt for Gold Tooth, grabbing his forearm in his teeth. The man screamed and rolled on the floor, the dog on top of him.

The other dog lunged for Nish, barking and using its paws to pin him against the stone wall.

"*I'm dead!*" Nish screamed. "*I'm dead!*"

The Malmö police quickly handcuffed the two Russians and lifted them to their feet, the boss limping badly and Gold Tooth still gasping for breath. Lars directed the police to the cell where the third mobster was still snoring.

One of the policemen had the *spangenhelm* and was examining it carefully. He whistled, and showed his superior, who said something to Lars.

Lars pointed to a dent on the side of the helmet, "The bullet did that," he said to Travis.

Travis couldn't believe it. *He had blocked a shot.*

It all took a while to sort out. More police came, then Muck and Mr. Dillinger, and then the two Russian bodyguards, looking more relieved than anyone. They raced up to Slava and grabbed him, kissing him on both cheeks.

Nish stared at them and rolled his eyes.

"*I'm gonna hurl!*" he said.

For once, Travis thought he might mean it.

Nish had been terrified by the dog, but when he heard why it had leapt for him, he was delighted. They had been hunting everywhere for the kids, but without luck. It wasn't until Data came up with the solution that the dogs were able to do their work.

Data had suggested the dogs follow the smell of Nish's hair. He had them sniff the mousse and gel that Nish had left in the bathroom, and within fifteen minutes the dogs had found the abandoned van and were headed towards the old castle.

A familiar call came from down the corridor.

"EEEE-AWWW-KEEE!"

It was Annika. She must have sneaked past the police line.

For once, Nish didn't answer. Instead, he turned, ducked down, and began pulling at his hair, trying to make it stand back up.

"*Who's got a comb?*" he hissed.

Lars handed one over. Nish frantically pulled and yanked and teased his hair, trying, without success, to make it stand back up in spikes.

He turned on Sarah, his eyes narrow, his nostrils flaring.

"You *ruined* my hair!" he said.

"Your hair saved our lives!" Sarah answered. "*Twice!*"

13

THEY'D DECIDED TO CONTINUE WITH THE tournament. The men had been arrested and the kids had all been checked out at the Malmö hospital. The swelling was already going down in Travis's eye, and Sarah's wrists had been dressed and wrapped in clean bandages.

Sarah and Travis had sat out the next game against Gothenburg, but Dmitri and Lars and Nish were cleared to play. Nish wouldn't have missed it for anything: a chance to be the hero in front of Annika and her friends.

The Gothenburg team had been excellent. They were all superb skaters, and most could handle the puck. But they weren't very big, especially compared to the bigger Owls like Andy, Wilson, and, of course, Nish. With Annika calling out every time he stepped on the ice, Nish had played like he was the size of Eric Lindros.

By the final period, the Owls had pulled away. Dmitri had scored twice and Nish once, on a shot from the point. After scoring, Nish had even pretended not to hear the yells from Annika and her friends, skating back out to centre with his stick over his knees and staring up at the clock to wait for the scoreboard to change. Travis and Sarah had to laugh.

"It's a wonder he doesn't stop and comb his hair," Sarah said.

Nish's goal had proven to be the winner. The Owls' record was two wins and a loss, which left them tied with two other teams for second place. The Owls, however, came out ahead, because they'd scored more goals. They were headed back to Stockholm for the championship. And they'd be playing the club with the best record in the tournament: CSKA, Slava Shadrin's team.

Travis Lindsay stood at the blueline and shook. He had never been so excited in his life. He was playing for the International Goodwill Pee Wee Championship – a *world* championship. As high as he could see in the massive Globen Arena, the red seats were filled with fans. *Thousands* of them! And everyone was standing for the anthems, first the Russian and then "O Canada." Travis shivered up the length of his spine.

He knew why so many people had come. The story was an international sensation. A thirteen-year-old hockey player had been kidnapped by the Russian mob. Other twelve- and thirteen-year-olds from Canada and Sweden had helped him escape. Lars Johanssen was a hero in Sweden. ("Maybe they'll put me on a stamp, like Peter Forsberg!" he joked.)

Sarah was insisting on playing – though her wrists had to be dressed again just before the game and she was obviously still in pain.

The big story, however, was Slava Shadrin. If he was good enough to be kidnapped by ruthless mobsters – *how good was he?* The stands of the Globen Arena were filled with the curious. There were even television cameras!

Nish was in his glory. He had worked on his hair half the afternoon. If Slava had thousands staring his direction, Nish knew that at least one in the crowd was staring only at him.

"Behind the net!" Travis had screamed over the cheers as the anthem ended. He was surprised to see Annika had come all the way from Malmö with some of her friends. They were waving a huge Canadian flag.

"Yeah," Nish said matter-of-factly. "I know."

Travis had never seen Muck look so relaxed before a big game. He was smiling, which was unusual. Muck wanted Sarah's line to start. "Remember," he said. "This is a 'goodwill' tournament – you're here to have fun. You're also representing your country.

"And one more thing," Muck said. He paused, grinning. "Don't even *think* about arguing with this referee."

Travis turned around. Across the ice the referee was stretching, one long leg extended to the side, his back to the Screech Owls' bench. But Travis didn't need to see the face to know who it was. The hair was enough.

Borje Salming!

Salming blew on his whistle to call the teams in for the opening face-off. He raised his hands to check the red lights at both ends. He smiled down on the two centres, Slava Shadrin and Sarah Cuthbertson, then winked at Travis.

Travis was in a state of shock as the puck fell.

Sarah won the face-off with her tricky little sweep move – pulling the puck out of the air just before it struck the ice – and before Travis knew it, it had rattled into his skate blades. He tried to kick the puck up to his stick so he could shoot it back to Nish, but he lost it in his skates and the Russian winger jabbed it loose and away.

Travis gave chase, but he was well behind the play. The winger hit a rushing defenceman, who clipped the puck off the glass so it skipped in behind Nish and, in an instant, was picked up by Slava Shadrin, cutting in like a sudden wind.

But so, too, was Sarah. There would be no quick goal this time. She laid her stick over Slava's and leaned hard, driving him off the puck before he could shoot. Data, racing over to cover up for Nish, picked up the puck and iced it. The linesman blew his whistle.

Sarah skated back to the bench shaking her right wrist. She wanted a change. Andy's line came out and Mr. Dillinger and Muck gathered round Sarah. She just nodded when they asked her if she felt all right. Nodded and stared straight ahead, over the boards. Travis, sitting beside her, wasn't convinced.

Ten minutes into the game, CSKA caught the Owls on a quick shift change. Slava Shadrin came over the boards and picked up a loose puck and beat Jesse Highboy easily. He came in on Wilson, beat him, and got past Jeremy with a high wrist shot that pinged in off the crossbar.

Russia 1, Canada 0.

Muck put a hand on Sarah's shoulder.

"Shadrin will kill us unless you stay with him," Muck said. "Are you up to it?"

"Yes."

"You're on, then."

Slava Shadrin's skates had barely hit the ice when the Russian star discovered he had grown a new shadow.

The opposing centres flew about the ice together like two sparrows in a field, Sarah turning precisely when Slava turned. If Slava picked up a loose puck or a pass, Sarah immediately checked him, using her stick on his and pushing down with all her strength so he could neither stickhandle nor pass. With Sarah on him, all Slava could do was dump the puck.

Travis was amazed. He had never seen anyone work as hard as Sarah. Sweat was pouring from her face. And he could tell from the way she winced and shook her gloves as she sat on the bench that she was in pain.

Travis saw Nish circling for the puck. He saw Nish's head come up for one quick look down the ice. Travis knew he wasn't looking for a place to pass the puck. He was looking for an opening.

Travis curled at the blueline, cutting across ice to his off wing. Dmitri read the play perfectly and moved to Travis's wing. Travis was now on the right, Dmitri on the left, as Nish broke straight up centre, carrying the puck.

Sarah saw what Nish was about to do, and she used her shoulder to ride Slava out of the play.

Slava's coach was leaning over the boards, shouting "Interference!" But no referee, not even Borje Salming, was going to call that. Sarah's pick was just a smart play.

Nish beat the first defence by letting the puck slide ahead and then quickly working his stick back and forth as if stickhandling. The defence-man fell for it and went for the stick blade, while the puck slid right by him and Nish looped around his side and was free.

It was now a three-on-one. Nish dropped the puck and ran right over the second Russian defenceman. More screams from the Russian bench. Dmitri picked up the loose puck and came in on their goaltender. He faked a shot and slipped the puck to Travis, flying in on his off wing. It was easy.

Canada 1, Russia 1.

It stayed that way until the break before the final period. Neither team could score. Slava couldn't get free of Sarah, and Nish couldn't lug the puck down the ice whenever he wanted any more. Both goaltenders were spectacular.

In the dressing room Travis could see that Sarah was in real pain. Her eyes welled up with tears just in taking off her gloves. The bandages were pink with bloodstains.

Mr. Dillinger had made ice-packs with plastic bags. He applied the ice and then carefully dressed the tortured wrists again.

"You okay to play?" Muck asked.

Sarah nodded. "I'm fine," she said. Travis noticed the little catch in her voice.

There was a knock at the door. Mr. Dillinger got it and signalled for Muck.

"The referee wants to talk to you," he said.

14

WHEN THE TWO TEAMS CAME OUT FOR THE final period, Muck and the Russian coach were still in deep discussion with Borje Salming. There were also two interpreters standing to the side, so it made for a tight little group in the corridor as the teams passed by. Every player was curious to know what was happening.

Then Salming and the coaches shook hands. All of them were smiling.

Nish, of course, was the one to ask: "What was all that about?"

"None of your business, Nishikawa."

Sarah and Slava lined up for the face-off. Travis could sense the tension. A 1–1 tie, Canada versus Russia, the peewee championship of the world – of the *universe*! – on the line.

Why, then, did Borje Salming seem to be chuckling as he raised his hand, a black glove covering the puck?

Slava and Sarah got set. Travis readied himself to jump into the play if Sarah tied up Slava.

Salming opened his hand and the puck fell.

The *little* puck!

Travis could hear Slava and Sarah gasp. He could hear Nish shout, "*What the —?*"

The puck bounced — and nothing was the same again.

Sarah lunged instinctively for the bouncing black disk and managed to tip it to Travis, who caught it perfectly on his blade.

It felt so comfortable! So tiny and small and light and . . . *alive*! Yes, that was it, *alive*!

Perhaps this was how a young basketball player would feel if his hand could hold a ball from above. Or a pitcher if the mound were moved a dozen steps closer to home plate.

Travis stickhandled quickly, the solid little puck dancing to the rhythm of his stick. He knew the Russian winger on his side was charging, but he knew as well that he had never felt more in control of a puck.

Travis spun, and the winger flew by, missing him. He snapped his stick and the puck flew back to Data, who caught it perfectly and fired it across ice to Nish, who was already in full motion.

Nish cradled the little puck as if it were an egg that would break if anyone so much as touched it as he passed by. He turned past the winger, then slipped the puck between Slava's feet and broke over centre, his head level, his hips square, the puck out in front of him and moving back and forth as if it were tied to the blade of his stick.

Soundless! Nish was stickhandling in utter silence, the puck soft on the stick blade, the ice so smooth from the flood there was only the sizzle and sigh of skates digging in and gliding.

Nish fired the little puck towards the far corner. It seemed to catch the wind, almost like a Frisbee as it hung in the air, and flew effortlessly, the rink suddenly filling with a loud crack as it found the glass and bounced back out, landing flat along the face-off circle.

Nish and Dmitri had played it perfectly. Dmitri had taken off the moment he figured Nish would dump the puck in. Dmitri was so fast he blew by the defence in a blur and was at the circle as the puck landed.

Dmitri was in and free – the shoulder fake, the move to the backhand, and the little puck clicked in smartly off the crossbar.

Canada 2, Russia 1.

"Is this legal?" Nish wanted to know when he had high-fived his way to the bench.

"We're here to have fun," Muck reminded him. "Remember?"

"Yeah, but . . . does it count if we use that little puck?"

"Did it go in?"

"Yeah, but –"

"Then it counts, Nishikawa. Relax."

Travis looked up at Muck and could hardly believe his eyes. Muck was laughing in the final period of a championship game, the Owls up by only one goal. He had never seen him so relaxed, so easygoing. And all because of a little puck.

Borje Salming faced the two teams off again, and again he dropped the miniature practice puck. It seemed he was going to finish the game with it. And why not? Travis said to himself. Look at how exciting the game has become.

The Russians tied it on a long shot from the point, the shot taking off so fast Travis couldn't even track it from the bench. Jeremy Weathers's glove shot out, but too late.

Russia 2, Canada 2.

Muck tapped Sarah on the shoulder the next time Slava's line came out. She went over the boards immediately, Dmitri and Travis following.

The face-off was in the Owls' end, to the right of Jeremy. Sarah wanted everyone placed exactly right, and while she was signalling to Nish, Jeremy skated quickly out to Travis.

"*No fair!*" Jeremy shouted.

Travis looked up. Jeremy was in despair. His face was red, flushed, and sweaty.

"Whadya mean?" Travis asked.

"I can't stop a puck I can't even see. You guys should have to use miniature sticks and wear skates that are two sizes too small."

Travis giggled at the thought. "Yeah, right."

The linesman blew quickly on his whistle and pointed to the net. Jeremy wiggled back. Travis looked down at the ice and laughed. He could hardly wait to get his stick on the little puck again. But he realized it wasn't the same for everyone. No doubt the Russian goalie felt the same as Jeremy. The goalies would prefer pucks the size of pizzas.

The puck flew back to the point, where one of the Russian defencemen gloved it and dropped it down for a perfect slapshot. Travis was the closest Owl. He knew what he had to do. He dived and twisted his body perfectly, the drive from the point hammering into his pants.

Compared with the danger he had faced this week, blocking a tiny puck seemed easy.

The two teams played back and forth for most of the period, neither side able to penetrate the other's defence. The miniature puck had such a strange effect on the game. The forwards were clearly more excited, trying harder, more anxious, and it caused a lot of broken plays. The defence were all more concerned, more wary of the power of a shot, and so they played with greater responsibility, always trying to make sure they kept shooters to the boards or blocked shots from the point. The goaltenders, too, seemed more alert, more worried, more frightened that they would let in a bad shot and be held responsible for a loss.

Travis figured he would have one final shift before the game ended. What would happen if the game was still tied? he asked himself. Overtime? A shootout?

They faced off to the left of Jeremy. Sarah won the puck from Slava and clipped it back to Nish, who immediately spun behind the net. Slava charged him. Nish tried a dangerous little move he had worked on in practice, a back pass against the boards just as the checker arrived, the puck bouncing back to Nish as the checker skated by. It worked perfectly! Nish faked to his right and broke out the left side, gathering speed.

Travis heard the call from behind the glass: "EEEE-AWWW-KEEE!"

Nish faked a pass to Dmitri and flipped a little backhand to Sarah, who was cutting across centre. Sarah carried the puck into the Russian end. She dropped for Dmitri, who tried to hit Travis flying in on the left side, but the defence stuck out his skate and the little puck ticked off and into the boards. Slava Shadrin, racing back, picked it up and turned. He failed, however, to see Nish sliding in to block any pass.

It was a dangerous pinch, but it worked. Nish's shin pads swept the little puck away from Slava, off the boards, and down into the corner, where Sarah was waiting. She shot the puck behind the net to Dmitri. Dmitri pivoted and fired it backhand out to Travis, who was fighting through the two defencemen to get to the front of the net.

Travis's stick blade just caught the little puck. It was so small, so light, that it stayed. He was off balance, falling, but he managed to flick a shot towards the net as he went down.

The tiny puck flew up as if Travis had cracked the hardest slapshot of his life. The goalie's glove shot out, but too late. The shot went hard into the roof of the net, exploding the goaltender's water bottle high into the air.

Travis knew it was in before he hit the ice. He couldn't believe it! He, Travis Lindsay, had just scored the winning goal against Russia in the final minute! He was Paul Henderson!

He felt the ice, hard beneath him, and he felt his teammates, soft but heavy as they piled on, screaming and screeching. The tangle of bodies and sticks and helmets slid towards the corner. The last to join in was a whooping Jeremy Weathers, who had skated the length of the ice to jump into the celebration.

"*Travis!*" they yelled.

"*Way to go, Trav!*"

"*We won!*"

"*We won!*"

"*We won!*"

15

THERE WERE THIRTY-FOUR SECONDS LEFT ON the clock, the same amount of time remaining when Paul Henderson had scored the goal to give Canada a win over the Soviet Union back in 1972. There was singing in the stands. Swedish flags and Canadian flags waving, everyone on their feet for the countdown. Travis could see Annika right against the glass in the Canadian end. She was blowing a kiss to Nish. Nish was pretending he hadn't noticed, leaning over with his stick on his knees and fussing with his skate laces. But Travis could see that, every once in a while, Nish was stealing a peek to check what was going on behind the glass.

Muck wanted Andy's line out for the final seconds. They were stronger defensively, but he also wanted Nish out with Lars, the two strongest Owls defencemen.

Travis drooped his glove over the boards and watched. His heart was still pounding. He was the hero, the Canadian hero, and he still couldn't believe it. He looked up towards the face-off circle, where Borje Salming was just moving in to drop the puck.

The little puck had barely hit the ice when the Russian centre bolted for the bench and Slava Shadrin leapt straight over the boards. One moment he was landing on the ice, the next he was a blur across the blueline. There was no time for Muck to get Sarah out!

Lars was a great skater, the best on the whole team at moving backwards or to the sides, but he was helpless against such speed.

Slava took the pass and looped around Lars. He came in on Jeremy, cutting across the crease. Jeremy lunged for the poke check just as Slava dropped the puck into his skates, then kicked it back up as Jeremy's stick bounced off Slava's shin pads. A quick little backhand and the puck was high in the far corner of the net.

Tie game!

"I can't shoot."

Travis said nothing. He, like everyone else, was listening to Sarah Cuthbertson explain to Muck why she couldn't take the first shot in the shootout. The two teams had played ten minutes of overtime without a goal being scored, and the reason was largely Sarah, who had checked Slava Shadrin so well he had not even managed one good shot on net.

But Sarah had paid a heavy price. Both her gloves were off. Mr. Dillinger had wrapped her wrists in towels, but the blood was seeping through. Sarah was crying. And if Sarah was crying, it had to hurt bad.

"Travis," Muck said. "You're up first."

Travis had half wanted this, half feared it. He was going to have to take the first shot for Canada. There was absolutely no doubt who would be taking the shot for Russia.

He took a deep breath and looked across the ice. Slava was already out, circling, staring down at the ice, gathering himself. Travis wondered how this must look to the huge crowd: Travis Lindsay, skinny, goofy Screech Owl, up against Slava Shadrin, the greatest peewee hockey player in the entire world.

Borje Salming was conferring with the two goaltenders. Travis could tell that Jeremy was talking excitedly. The Russian goalie also seemed worked up. Borje Salming was nodding. Salming skated over to the Russian bench, talked with the coach, then came over and spoke to Muck.

"The goalies want to go back to the regulation puck for the shootout," he explained. "It's only fair."

"No problem," Muck said. He obviously wanted Jeremy to have every chance possible.

They would shoot in turn, starting with Slava and Travis. Then four more shooters for each team would follow. If the teams were still tied after five shots each, they would go into a sudden-death shootout, beginning again with the first two, Travis Lindsay for Canada, and Slava Shadrin for Russia.

Slava went first. He flew down the ice so fast Jeremy had trouble moving with him, and when he passed by, he reached back and tapped the puck into the open far side. A goal so seemingly effortless that Jeremy slammed his stick in anger against the crossbar. But all the Owls knew how impossible it had been. It was a great goal.

Borje Salming laid the puck at centre ice and blew the whistle for Travis to begin skating.

Travis felt like he was sneaking up on the puck. And when he reached it, it seemed the puck had grown to the size of a patio stone. It was as if it weighed more than he did. His arms were weak, his legs rubbery. He felt like he was once again wearing the *spangenhelm* and his neck muscles were giving way. He moved up over the blueline slowly, afraid even to stickhandle for fear he would drop the huge, heavy puck and skate right past it.

Should he deke? Shoot? He didn't know and hadn't any time to decide. He was instantly at the edge of the net, trying to put a backhand through the solid mass of the goalie's pads, not a crack of daylight between the goalie and the post.

The puck dribbled off harmlessly to the side.

The Russian bench went crazy. Half the crowd cheered and whistled and sang. Travis skated, head down, back to his bench. No one looked at him.

The second shooters both failed, and so, too, did the third.

When the fourth Russian shooter failed, Muck chose Lars Johanssen to take the shot for Canada. It was a surprising move — *a defenceman?* — but Travis understood. They couldn't use their best player, Sarah. And Dmitri had already shot and just missed a high corner. Lars had moves. And Lars was in his home country, with his family in the stands.

He came up the ice slowly, almost as if he were sitting in a chair relaxing. He didn't seem afraid of stickhandling the big puck. He slowed up even more, seemed almost to stop, then accelerated quickly, catching the goalie for a second off guard. The goaltender moved with him, and Lars reached back with one hand on his backhand and tapped the puck in.

Tied, again!

The Canadian bench emptied and piled onto Lars. Travis was one of the first to reach him, and they went down together under a crush of bodies.

"*Way to go, Lars!*" Travis screamed.

"*I tried my Peter Forsberg!*" Lars shouted back, ecstatic.

The fifth Russian was stopped by a great butterfly move by Jeremy, leaving one final Canadian chance in the first round of the shootout. But who was going to take it?

"Nishikawa," Muck said.

Nish skated all the way back to the Canadian net and slammed Jeremy on the pads. He took off his helmet and skated to the glass, leaned into it, and left a big smudge of a kiss for Annika. The crowd roared and cheered.

Nish then came flying down the ice and picked up the puck at centre. He hit the Russian blueline – everyone thinking deke – and suddenly wound up and let go the wildest, hardest slapper Travis had ever seen, a shot so hard that the follow-through knocked Nish to the ice.

The shot hit the goalie's glove and kept going, the puck like a live mouse as it scurried up over the edge of the Russian's glove and found the net.

Nish, still sliding along the ice on his back, hit the goalie next, the two of them crashing into the net with the puck.

Borje Salming's whistle was in his mouth, and his cheeks were puffing in and out, but Travis couldn't hear. He could see Salming's hand though, and Salming was pointing into the net.

Goal!

Canada wins!

16

IF HOCKEY KEPT SUCH RECORDS, THIS WOULD have gone down as the greatest pile-on in history. The second the red light went on, the Screech Owls poured onto the ice like a pail of minnows dumped off the end of a dock.

Travis felt as if he had left the ice surface at the blueline and hadn't landed until he was at the crease, his stick and gloves and helmet flying as he soared and slid towards the greatest Canadian hero of the moment: Wayne Nishikawa.

"*Hey!*" Nish screamed as the first Screech Owls hit him. "*Watch the hair!*"

But no one paid him the slightest attention. Dmitri pushed off Nish's helmet, Lars wrapped his arms around him, Sarah — trying to protect her bleeding wrists — fell onto him, laughing.

"*The hair! The hair!*" Nish screamed.

Even Muck piled on. In all the dozens of tournaments the Owls had played, Travis had never seen Muck do much more than smile or nod or, a couple of times, shake the hands of the players as they came off the ice. But Muck was digging down from on top, his big face open wide in a laugh that had no sound.

Muck found what he was looking for: Nish's head. He grabbed it in a hammerlock, then sharply rasped the knuckles of his free hand through Nish's pride and joy.

"Not my hair! Lemme go!"

Travis could see Nish's beet-red face from where he lay in the tangle. He could tell the last thing in the world Nish wanted was to be let go. He was the hero of the hour – and he was going to milk it for all it was worth.

Travis felt a body pushing up from beneath him. He thought at first it must be Sarah, trying to protect her wrists, but when he turned he realized it was the little Russian goaltender, still trapped in the Owls' pile-on.

The goalie was crying. Travis could see through the player's mask that his eyes were red and swollen and wet. It must have been horrible for him; not only had he let in the goal that lost the tournament, but then he had been forced to be part of the celebration.

They hugged Nish and roughed up his greasy hair and slapped his shoulders and his back, and finally the knot of legs and arms and heads undid itself and the Owls began collecting their gloves and sticks and helmets for the post-tournament ceremony.

Dmitri's stick was over by Travis's left glove. As they bent down, Travis asked a quick question.

"How do you say, 'Great game'?"

Dmitri looked up. "'Great game.' Just like that."

"No, no, I mean in Russian."

"Oh. . . . Try, '*Horoshosvgeal.*'"

"'*Horse-os* . . .'"

Dmitri shook his head, laughing. "'*Horosh-osv-geal,*'" he repeated carefully.

"'*Horoshosvgeal.*'"

"That's it."

They lined up for the handshake. Jeremy went first, Travis last, then Muck. The Russians were very gracious, some of them smiling. Travis came to the goalie who'd been crying and reached out with his arm and grabbed the goalie's shoulder instead of his hand and brought him to a stop.

"'*Horoshosvgeal,*'" Travis said.

The goalie stopped. He blinked, his eyes still red. Then he smiled.

Travis came to Slava, who hit Travis on the shoulder and smiled when he saw him.

"'*Horoshosvgeal,*'" Travis said.

Slava looked back, then roared with laughter.

"Thank you," he said in English. "And the same to you!"

Slava came to Sarah, who couldn't shake hands because of her wrists. He smiled, and suddenly –

much to Sarah's shock – grabbed her in a big bear hug, lifting her off the ice. The rest of the CSKA players rattled their sticks on the ice in recognition. Perhaps better than anyone, they knew the job Sarah had done on Slava.

Some of the crowd was on the ice. Annika and her Swedish friends came running and sliding and cheering over to the Owls. Annika jumped at Nish and wrapped herself around his neck. They hugged, but Travis noticed there was no kiss. Nish obviously felt safer with a half-inch of bulletproof Plexiglas between them.

The tournament organizers had rolled out a red carpet for the final ceremonies.

Two young women followed behind Borje Salming carrying medals on velvet cushions.

One by one Salming placed a medal around the neck of each Screech Owl and shook the player's hand. When Sarah couldn't shake, he leaned over and gave her a gentle kiss on the cheek, which brought a cheer from the crowd.

Borje Salming came to Travis and smiled as he put the medal around his neck. "Good game," he said as he shook Travis's hand.

Travis was speechless.

Nish was standing next to Travis. Salming gave him his medal, shook his hand, and then patted his shoulder.

"Good defenceman," Borje Salming said. "Just like me."

Nish, of course, was never speechless: "We have the same hair," he said.

Borje Salming looked at Nish as if he had lost his mind. Nish just stood there, grinning.

"Hey," Nish said, when Salming had moved along, "I had to say *something*, didn't I?"

Silver medals were awarded to the Russian team and then the bronze to the Djurgårdens peewee team that had come in third. They then announced the Most Valuable Player for each team. Slava Shadrin won for CSKA and the crowd gave a huge cheer as Mr. Johanssen made the presentation. The Russian delegation then came out onto the carpet and the Most Valuable Player for Canada was announced.

"*Wayne Nishikawa!*"

Nish looked startled. He dropped his stick and gloves and began skating over, but suddenly stopped. He was right in front of Sarah.

"This should have been yours," he said.

Sarah smiled. "You scored the winner," she said graciously.

Nish smiled back. "You got us into the shootout."

The Russian leader handed him a wrapped present, and Nish took it and then reached out his hand to shake.

The man shook his head. He leaned over instead and kissed Nish on one cheek. Then he went for the other but missed as a startled Nish jumped back, a look of shock on his face.

The Russian laughed and shook his head.

Nish stopped again as he passed Sarah. He handed her the MVP award. "I wish you'd won it in the first place," he said, trying to wipe his cheek with the sleeve of his Owls sweater.

The Globen Arena burst into wild cheers.

Behind Travis, Annika screeched: "EEEE-AWWW-KEEE!"

They then stood by the thousands in Stockholm's Globen Arena. And at the far end of the rink a red-and-white Canadian flag began its long climb up a guy wire towards the rafters.

Travis was barely aware that the anthem had begun, but soon it seemed as if the music of "O Canada" had filled the huge stadium and was pounding in his heart. Behind the great swell of music, he could hear people singing along. The Canadian parents . . . then more and more of the Swedes.

It was the most beautiful sound he had ever heard.

There was another sound a bit behind him. It was a sort of low drone, but growing louder.

He turned slightly to his left. It was Nish, singing off-key, his eyes staring straight up at the flag.

Nish was crying. Big, fat tears were burning down his cheek and falling freely onto his sweater. He was singing and crying at the same time, and he didn't seem to care the slightest that he couldn't sing a note.

THE END

Mystery at Lake Placid

Travis Lindsay, his best friend, Nish, and all their pals on the Screech Owls hockey team, are on their way to New York State for an international peewee tournament. Excitement builds in the team van on their way to Lake Placid. First there are the entertaining antics of their trainer, Mr. Dillinger – then there's the prospect of playing on an Olympic rink, in a huge arena, knowing there will be scouts in the stands.

But they have barely arrived when things start to go wrong. Their star player, Sarah, plays badly from lack of sleep. Next Travis gets knocked down in the street. And then someone starts tampering with their equipment. It looks as if someone is trying to sabotage the Screech Owls. But who? And why? And can Travis and the others stop the destruction before the decisive game of the tournament?

Terror in Florida

When Travis, Nish, Sarah, and the rest of the gang pile onto a school bus headed for Florida, the Screech Owls are anticipating a spring break with a little sun, a little sand, and lots of ice! With some luck, they may even make the peewee tournament final, to be held in the Ice Palace, home of the Tampa Bay Lightning!

It looks like it's going to be a fun trip. Muck and Mr. Dillinger are taking them to Disney World and to an alligator farm and to go swimming in the ocean. Nish, of course, has bigger ideas. With his new X-ray glasses he bought on the "Stupid Stop" on the way down, he's hoping to see more than anyone has ever seen on a trip to Florida.

The only trouble is, Nish ends up seeing too much! Travis wasn't looking forward to riding the Tower of Terror at MGM Studios, but it's going to take even more courage to face the terror Nish has just uncovered. His best friend has stumbled upon a plot to terrorize all of America!

THE SCREECH OWLS SERIES